THE ASSIGNMENT

Evangeline Anderson

Prologue

Early 1980s

"This is gonna take some getting used to." Detective Sean O'Brian plopped down on the huge, four-poster, king-sized bed and slid one hand up the elaborately carved post nearest him thoughtfully. "Lap of luxury," he muttered.

"What, sleeping in the same bed, or being my 'boy'?" Detective Nicholas Valenti, O'Brian's partner of six years, grinned at the smaller man while he stowed his folded clothes in the carved oak dresser that matched the bed. O'Brian was done with that chore, having shoveled his own clothes into the two drawers above Valenti's the minute they walked into the room.

Usually O'Brian was the neatnik, while Valenti tended to let things go, but the tall man felt the need to have something to do with his hands. As for O'Brian's hasty unpacking job -- well, Valenti reflected, it wasn't the first thing his partner had done out of character lately -- not by a long shot. The fact that they were unpacking their bags at the RamJack was ample proof of that.

"Both," O'Brian said succinctly. "But I still don't understand why *I* have to be *your* boy. Why can't I be the sugar-daddy, huh? I'm butch enough."

Valenti sighed. Not *this* again. He was beginning to think that O'Brian was whining about their arrangement just to get to him. A small smile playing around the corners of his partner's full mouth told him his guess was probably correct.

"We agreed that you would be the boy because you're so little and cute and furry -- like a blond teddy bear, remember?" He looked over his shoulder and grinned at O'Brian, who had flopped onto his back, the better to enjoy the plush mattress.

Valenti knew his partner hated to be teased about his blond good looks and compact stature. O'Brian wasn't exactly short at five-nine, but he wasn't exactly tall, either, especially compared with Valenti's six-two. "Also, because you're better at shaking your ass," Valenti added.

"You got that right." O'Brian grinned back, refusing to rise to the bait. The grin reaching all the way up to his sea-green eyes, fringed thickly with reddish-blond lashes. "Yeah, I know I'm cute, and I'll play your boy. Just don't expect me to suck your dick, all right?"

"I think I can safely promise it won't come to that," Valenti answered dryly. But his partner's words caused something low in his body to tense. "After all," he continued, trying to put O'Brian's careless words out of his mind as he shoved the rest of his socks in the drawer, "Captain Harris told us to go undercover -- not *under* the *covers.*"

"Yeah, yeah, I know. Remind me again how we got such a plum assignment," O'Brian grumbled. He rolled over on the bed so that he lay on his stomach and looked at his partner in the mirror over the dresser. "Oh, yeah -- 'cause none of the Narc detectives that *should* be doin' this job are comfortable enough together to play 'gay.' But apparently we are."

"You have to admit, O'Brian, we don't freak out if we accidentally touch each other, like a lot of guys do." Valenti caught himself noticing in the mirror how tightly his partner's jeans were stretched over his firm ass and had to look down quickly at the drawer he was filling so methodically.

"That's 'cause we're so studly, we don't have to worry. We're secure in our masculinity, *corazón. Muy macho,*" O'Brian answered contentedly. It was a joke between them that the Irish O'Brian knew more Spanish than his partner. Valenti couldn't speak a word despite the fact that he looked every inch of his Colombian heritage, with his black hair, brown eyes, and natural tan. He was actually more WASP than Latino in temperament and background.

"Yeah, we're a regular couple of studs, all right," Valenti answered distractedly, still unpacking. "Wish you wouldn't call me that, Sean."

O'Brian had always had a penchant for crazy nicknames, and he had picked up the affectionate Spanish *corazón*, which meant "heart," from Valenti's grandmother on a trip back east to visit his best friend's family a few years before.

Abuelita was the only member of Valenti's family to retain her ethnicity in the move his parents had made from the south side of the Bronx to the Hamptons when Valenti's father had made it big. Valenti had only been three at the time, and his upwardly mobile father had insisted that nothing but English would ever be spoken in his new home.

So aside from a few standard phrases and his grandmother's pet name for him, Valenti didn't speak a word of Spanish. O'Brian, who had no formal training but a natural ear for languages, did.

"What, corazón? You know you love it, Valenti. Besides, what are you afraid of -- that people are gonna get the wrong idea about us? In this place, it'd be the *right* idea, ya know?" O'Brian laughed, a musical tenor that always fooled people into thinking he had a beautiful singing voice. Valenti knew the truth about that -- his partner might have an ear for languages, but he was completely tone-deaf when it came to music. O'Brian couldn't carry a tune in a bucket.

"I should never have let you know I hated that nickname," Valenti grumbled, still trying not to look in the mirror. Honestly, he didn't see how the hell O'Brian's jeans stayed on at all. He wore them so tight over his round, firm ass, they always seemed in imminent danger of spontaneous combustion -- the way Valenti felt any time he was around his partner lately. Since he and O'Brian were almost always around each other, it was creating something of a problem for him.

"Make ya a deal: I promise not to call you by your abuelita's nickname for you, if you'll just hurry the hell up with the unpacking. I wanna go check this place out -- it's s'posed to be really ritzy." O'Brian sat up suddenly on the bed.

"Almost done. Can't wait to get out there and shake your groove thang, huh, partner?" Valenti answered, trying to get back to their normal banter. He risked a look in the mirror and saw his own worried eyes looking back.

"You know it babe -- I'm hot." O'Brian jumped off the bed and did a few impromptu dance steps to prove it, shaking his round ass for the benefit of Valenti and thousands of adoring invisible fans.

Valenti shook his head in mock exasperation. This was the first really big case they'd been assigned since O'Brian's near-fatal stabbing over six months ago, and his partner was a ball of nervous energy.

"Get outta here," he growled, slapping O'Brian on the back with a folded undershirt. "Go explore on your own for a while and leave me to finish unpacking in peace. Just try to stay out of trouble, and I'll meet you later."

"You sure you wanna risk some other daddy bear grabbin' my tender virgin ass when you're not there to protect me?" O'Brian grinned and batted surprisingly long eyelashes. He stripped off his leather jacket, revealing the familiar furry chest underneath a skin-tight white T-shirt.

Twonnie, their consultant about all things gay, had tried his best to convince O'Brian to wax, arguing that gay men in general and boy toys in particular didn't go for that much body hair. But O'Brian had adamantly refused. Secretly, Valenti was glad about that -- his partner wouldn't have been the same without the mat of wiry, reddish-gold hair that decorated his well-defined chest.

Still posing for his fans, O'Brian preened for the mirror. "I'm a hot little twinkie." The skin-tight jeans clung lovingly to his plush ass and outlined his heavy cock, which bulged suggestively through the worn material.

Valenti groaned and rolled his eyes in mock disgust, although he privately agreed with his partner's assessment of his own body. "Would you get outta here?" He shook his head sarcastically. "You're driving me nuts with your blatant sexuality." In fact, he was more than half hard from watching his partner move so provocatively, but he kept up their usual casual banter, hoping O'Brian wouldn't notice. There was no reason for his partner to be looking at his crotch anyway. O'Brian didn't swing that way, no matter what Valenti had been wishing lately.

"I'm goin' already." O'Brian threw one last grin over his shoulder as he sashayed to the door of their suite in that hip-rolling, ass-shaking swagger he had perfected for this assignment. "But you're gonna miss me when I'm gone."

"Yeah, I'll miss you like a bad rash," Valenti said lamely and made as if to throw a pair of rolled-up socks at his partner's head. Pretending to duck, O'Brian scooted out the door quickly, only to open it a second later, poking his head through the crack to say, "See ya later -- *daddy*." The socks hit the door as he banged it shut with a flourish, and Valenti could hear him laughing all the way down the hall of the luxurious resort.

Valenti closed his eyes and sank onto the plush surface of the bed, his broad shoulders hunched in defeat. He had a bad feeling about this assignment. A feeling that it could alter their partnership forever. He wondered again how he and O'Brian had ever let themselves be talked into going undercover in the country's largest gay resort.

His mind flashed back to the scene in Captain Harris's office a week ago...

Chapter Two

"Got something for you two." Harris was quieter than usual, almost subdued, Valenti thought. He studied their captain, waiting to hear what he wanted. Harris's usually neat gray hair was rumpled as though he had been running both hands through it, and his red-and-yellow "power tie" was pulled loose so that the knot hung a good three inches below his collar. It was an unheard-of informality in a man who valued an orderly personal appearance.

"Yeah?" Beside him, O'Brian slouched easily on the arm of Valenti's chair rather than getting one of his own, legs spread wide to give his heavy cock more room in the skin-tight pants he habitually wore. He had one arm thrown around his partner's shoulders in a comradely fashion.

Valenti knew the picture they must present to anyone passing by the big glass window of Harris's office -- the dark head and the light, closer than they ought to be if you listened to the dictates of a homophobic society, which he and O'Brian never did. Coming from a large, affectionate Irish family, O'Brian was a touchy-feely guy. He was comfortable displaying affection and always had been, ever since the two men had met in the LAPD Police Academy and become instant friends.

Valenti had come to California on his own private exodus. He had been trying to get away from his controlling father, who couldn't believe his son would rather be a cop than a doctor or a lawyer or a broker or any of the other "respectable" professions that his family's wealth and privilege demanded. O'Brian had been a smart-mouthed Irish kid fresh out of the army.

They had been a perfect match right from the start, complementing each other's strengths and shoring up each other's weaknesses. The Ivy-League-educated Valenti had been top of their class academically, while O'Brian had led in physical aptitude and was a deadly marksman. They had become inseparable, dubbed "The Mick and the Spic," and the gag at the academy was that they were only one ethnic group away from a pretty good joke. But the way Captain Harris was looking at them now, Valenti tended to think that the case he was about to assign was no laughing matter.

"Yeah," Harris said shortly, finally acknowledging O'Brian's one-word question. He was playing with a yellow number-two pencil nervously, moving it between his fingers and thumbs as he spoke. "Something from Narcotics, actually, but there's nobody in their department can handle it. You guys heard about the kid who OD'd down at the Dancing Queen last week?"

"On coke, right?" Valenti asked. The Dancing Queen was a notorious gay night spot downtown that was constantly being raided for illegal drugs and yet somehow still managed to stay open. The overdose Harris was talking about was the fourth one that month, and every one had involved large doses of cocaine.

"Uh-huh. A shitload of it, cut with something toxic -- possibly rat poison. Heavy-duty stuff and very dangerous. We raided the place again last night and got a supplier. He agreed to talk in return for immunity, so we cut a deal. Now we know where the stuff is coming from, and we have an idea who the guy behind it is. Name is Vincent Conrad, and he's been in the drug scene a long time."

"So you need someone to go undercover and make the bust," O'Brian finished for him. "But why us, Cap'n? Ain't Narc got enough guys without draggin' our asses outta Homicide? Valenti an' me were getting' so comfortable." He gave his partner's shoulder a friendly squeeze. Valenti smiled humorlessly. He'd been anything but comfortable around his partner lately, and what department he was in had nothing to do with it.

"Well, yes, but I don't think any of them is as qualified to handle the situation as you two are." Harris looked distinctly ill at ease, and the pencil he had been playing with suddenly snapped in his hands. "You see..." He studied the two pencil halves carefully, as though thinking of gluing them back together, before placing them on his desk. "The guy we want has his headquarters in 'Frisco."

"Ah, good ol' San Fran, city of brotherly love." O'Brian grinned at his partner, and Valenti grinned back uneasily, wondering where this was headed.

"Uh, I think that's Philadelphia you're thinking of, O'Brian," he said.

"Nope, Philly don't have nothin' on the City by the Bay when it comes to that kind of action -- or so I hear," his partner said, looking back at their captain. "So, he's in 'Frisco and you want us to make the bust. But you still didn't say why us."

Valenti was already beginning to get a bad feeling, and it only deepened when Harris cleared his throat and said, "Conrad has his headquarters at a resort he owns -- the RamJack."

"What?" Valenti couldn't keep the apprehension out of his voice. "You're saying you want us to go undercover at the biggest gay resort in the country?" The RamJack was so notorious that even outside the gay community it had a reputation for decadence and corruption.

He half expected his partner to explode at the suggestion, but O'Brian just lay even further back on the arm of his partner's chair. There was a dangerous glint in his sea-green eyes, and

Valenti watched them change to a flat, hard emerald when he addressed their captain.

"And what makes you think Valenti and I would be so good at this assignment, Cap'n?" he asked, his voice dangerously low and cool. "You sayin' Valenti and I are gay?"

Valenti could understand his partner's defensiveness. He knew there had been rumors about them before because of their close friendship and the way they were so comfortable in each other's space. Rumor was one thing, but to hear their captain say they should play a gay couple because they were more "suited" for the part than any other detective team was something else. *Talk about damning us with faint praise*, Valenti thought sourly.

"No, hell, no!" Harris blustered furiously, finding another pencil to bend. "But, well...damn it, O'Brian, you two are just more *comfortable* around each other than any other detectives we've got. You've been partners a long time -- you *know* each other. And you're not a pair of rabid homophobes like a lot of the guys here. Who am I gonna send, huh? Jenkins and Johnson? Jenkins snickers like a schoolboy every time he sees a drag queen, and Johnson would lose his lunch if I asked him to stay at a gay resort -- let alone pretend to be gay himself. And the rest are just as bad or worse.

"No." Harris shook his head. "You two are my only option. I know it's awkward, but that can't be helped. Of course..." He put the pencil down on his desk blotter beside the broken one and leaned back in his chair. "...you two can refuse the assignment. Technically it's out of our jurisdiction, so it's strictly voluntary."

"But this Conrad is putting some heavy-duty shit on the street, and kids are getting killed because of it. I'd really like to nail this bastard, and I thought you'd agree with me."

"We'll do it," O'Brian said, at the same time Valenti said, "No way," emphatically. They looked at each other, confused. They were almost always in agreement.

Harris looked at both of them and frowned. Valenti knew what he was thinking -- O'Brian should be the one having a problem with this assignment, *not* his partner.

Everyone knew that despite being so touchy-feely, O'Brian was the more macho of the two men. Valenti knew that his partner's upbringing probably had something to do with that. Growing up in one of the toughest blue-collar Irish-Catholic neighborhoods in Boston, and being short and blond, with features that were so finely molded they were almost pretty, had given O'Brian something to prove. Valenti was more easygoing -- more willing to keep an open mind about things like this. But, then, he hadn't had to fight every dumb jock in his neighborhood that called him a "fucking faggot" growing up because he was small and cute, either.

Captain Harris just sighed and shook his head. "Talk it out and let me know. Got to have both of you on board for this one to work." Harris motioned for them to leave. "Shut the door behind you, and let me know by the end of the day," he said, turning back to the paperwork on his desk.

Outside the office, the partners argued in lowered voices.

"What's with you, O'Brian? I thought this kind of thing made you sick. Why the sudden change of heart?"

Valenti was genuinely baffled. O'Brian had never been one of those cops that went in for gay bashing, but he had never been exactly gay-friendly, either. Valenti usually ended up dealing with their few homosexual informants. And ever since O'Brian's little brother, Ian, had left his wife and three young children for his insurance salesman, homosexuality -- especially man-on-man homosexuality -- had been a touchy subject. Valenti sometimes thought it was Ian's duplicity more than his sexuality that bothered O'Brian, but it still wasn't something they talked about very much or very easily.

"What's with *you*, Valenti?" O'Brian demanded, without answering his partner's question. "You never struck me as a homophobe. Thought you were a real open-minded kinda guy."

"I *am* open-minded, but Sean, we don't know what we're getting into here," Valenti protested, knowing it sounded lame, but unable to come up with a better excuse. There was no way he was going to give the real reason for his reluctance to accept the mission, given his partner's usual take on the gay lifestyle.

O'Brian snorted dismissively. "Yeah, I do -- we're gonna go in there and nail the scum that's been handing out poisoned candy to every twinkie in town. Ya know, Valenti, I may not agree with the lifestyle, but they got a right to live, same as you and me."

"I know. It's just..." Valenti floundered, completely unable to find the words. "Well, the captain's right -- we *are* more comfortable around each other than the other guys, but still -- we're only comfortable up to a point, you know?"

"Aw, whatza matter, Nicky, afraid you'll have to hold my hand?" O'Brian made light of it, but there was an angry glint in his eye.

He thinks I don't want him -- don't want to touch him that way, Valenti thought despairingly. *God help me, if only he knew...*

"It's not that, and you know it," he said quietly. "It's just...aw, hell, Sean, I don't know. You don't think it'll be weird?"

"Not if we don't let it bother us," his partner replied, lightening up and clapping Valenti on the back. "It's just another undercover assignment, Nick, that's all. Now come on -- you in or out?"

"In, I guess," Valenti replied, feeling like a drowning man going down for the third time. He wondered if it was O'Brian's use of his first name that made him agree; his partner only called him Nick when he was really serious about something.

"Great." O'Brian's face lit up, and his eyes were deep sea green again. "I'll go tell Harris. We're gonna nail this scum, partner. You wait and see."

"As long as *we* don't get nailed in the process," Valenti said. He had meant to be sarcastic, but his words came out quiet and a little sad. O'Brian looked at him strangely and shook his head.

"Don't worry, Valenti. Nobody's goin' down but Conrad. Hey, it's us-against-them time -- the Mick and the Spic against the forces of evil. Who do ya think's gonna win? Gotta be us, right?" He winked and ran one hand through his thick thatch of reddish-blond hair.

"Right," Valenti returned dutifully. He wondered why, if the outcome was so certain, he felt such a sense of foreboding as his partner turned and walked with jaunty steps back to Harris's office.

"We'll take it," he heard O'Brian say. "So when do we leave?"

Chapter Three

"A project like this, you got to do some research. Got to e-du-cate yourselves, you know?"

They were sitting in the ShySide bar, talking with their good friend and best information source, Turk. Turk was a huge black man with a head as bald and shiny as a billiard ball, and enough muscles to crush anyone who was stupid enough to get on his bad side. He was the owner of the ShySide and regularly wore color combinations that would make a blind man cry. But he always had the latest news on the streets, and his information was never wrong.

Today Turk was dressed to the nines in lime-green pants and a bright pink shirt. The outfit made Valenti think of a psychedelic watermelon, and the white slice of a smile that split Turk's face almost lightened his mood. Almost.

"Hey, we didn't come here to ask for advice on how to work the case, Turk," O'Brian replied, grinning to show he was kidding. "We came for information. I mean, me and Valenti been in and outta the gay bars on different cases often enough to know what's going down in there."

"Yeah, but every time you been there, it was as cops, not as *patrons*," Turk pointed out. "I'm just sayin', it wouldn't hurt you to go down to one of those bars and just hang out. Ob-*serve* the regulars and get some per-*spec*-tive, if you see what I'm saying."

"We'll think about it. Now, you know anything about Vincent Conrad or the RamJack?"

"What I don't know, I can find out." Turk smiled again. "But what I do know, you are *not* going to like."

Valenti closed his eyes and groaned out loud. *What next?*

"What's wrong with him?" Turk asked O'Brian, jerking his head at Valenti.

"Ah, don't mind tall, dark, and gloomy there -- he's afraid we're not up to the challenge of actin' Mary enough to fool the other Marys. Like it's gonna be so hard."

"Might be more to it than you think," Turk warned again. "I'm telling you, my man, ed-u-*ca*-tion is the key."

"I just think we might have bitten off more than we can chew, O'Brian." Valenti said desperately. "I mean, Turk's right -- what do we know about acting gay?"

"Apparently more than the other guys down at the Metro," O'Brian shot back impatiently. "Or Harris wouldn't have laid this one in our laps. Now, come on, Valenti, get with the program." He turned back to Turk. "No more chit-chat, T -- spill it. What do you know about Conrad and the RamJack off the top of your head?"

"Well, normally I wouldn't know too much about that scene, you understand. But it just so happens I have a cousin, Antwon, who swings that way. He's stayed at the RamJack on several occasions, courtesy of a good friend of his, if you know what I mean. In fact..." He snapped his thick brown fingers in excitement. "Antwon would be the best person to tell you all about it. Everything I know is secondhand from him. I'll call him up, get him to meet you at his favorite hangout tonight. Then he can help *ed*-u-cate you boys. What do you say?"

"Fine," O'Brian said at the same time Valenti said, "What's his favorite hangout?"

Turk grinned widely again. "Why, the Dancing Queen, of course. My man likes to shake a leg once in a while -- among other things."

"Oh, geez..." Valenti was shaking his head, but his partner looked thoughtful.

"Might not be a bad idea after all -- return to the scene of the crime an' all." He raised an eyebrow. "What do you think, Valenti?"

"Why not?" Valenti asked sarcastically. "After all, we're going to be undercover for God knows how long at a huge gay resort next week, but that's not soon enough for you. Nooo -- you have to start taking us to gay bars now. So I say, sure, let's go. I can't *wait*."

"What's with you lately?" O'Brian gripped his shoulder and leaned in to peer into his partner's eyes. "You haven't been yourself the past couple weeks -- don't think I haven't noticed, babe. Somethin' you wanna talk about? You don't have to keep it all bottled up inside, ya know -- not when you got me to talk to."

His partner's warm hand on his shoulder caused Valenti to shiver. O'Brian was so *close*. He could smell the warm musk of the other man's skin and see the deep-green eyes so filled with concern, and those perfect, full lips almost near enough to kiss... He pulled away and turned to lean on the counter.

"It's nothing," he said. "Just got a lot on my mind lately, you know? Sorry if I got out of line, Sean."

"Nah, that's okay." Sean smiled sympathetically and gave him a quick, spontaneous hug before pulling away. "I understand. Keep it to yourself if you want, Nick. Just know I'm here when you're ready to talk."

Valenti shook his head mutely; he would never be able to talk about what was bothering him -- not to his partner, anyway...

* * *

It had come to him nearly a month ago as they sat in an unmarked car on yet another endless stakeout -- a name for the slowly growing emotion he had been feeling since that horrible night O'Brian had been stabbed. Love.

It had fallen on his head from out of the blue, like a meteor with his name on it. So many days and nights spent watching his partner recover from the near-fatal wounds. The way their relationship had grown in that time as they excluded everyone from their circle of two. O'Brian had been intent on getting well, and Valenti had been intent on doing everything in his power to heal him.

It was as though his subconscious could no longer keep its secret, and it came bursting through in a conscious thought that took him completely by surprise. Valenti had been watching his partner watch the house where their perp was known to hang out, when suddenly he'd thought: *I love him.*

He tried to push it away, of course; he didn't feel that way about men. Never had before, anyway. He tried to explain it as something else. *Of course I love him -- he's my best friend, my go-to guy. My partner. I'd trust him with my life and take a bullet in a heartbeat to save him. That's what love is, isn't it?*

He thought of all the things they'd been through together -- all the rough times he wouldn't have made it through without Sean Michael O'Brian. The way he had fallen apart after his wife, Madeline, had left him, when O'Brian had been the only one who could hold him together, leapt readily to mind as well. Not to mention the numerous times his partner had saved his ass on the streets.

But that wasn't it, or not all of it, anyway. That was love, sure -- the love of one good friend for another. But it didn't explain why he suddenly wanted to reach out and run his fingers through that wild thatch of reddish-blond hair or hold O'Brian in his arms. Or caress that smooth, golden skin and kiss that full, red mouth...

The sudden desire bloomed in his chest like an alien rose that had been sprouting stealthily for months, maybe years. It was utterly unfamiliar to him, but completely undeniable -- he *wanted* his partner. Wanted him sexually. *I don't just love him*, he'd thought with something like despair. *I'm in love with him. And there's not a damn thing I can do about it.*

The knowledge was like a weight tied to his legs, and Nicholas Valenti felt he was drowning slowly, a little more every day. Drowning in his partner's easy, casual affection -- an arm around his shoulders here, a hug there. Harris was right about them; they were comfortable with each other -- maybe *too* comfortable, Valenti thought miserably, trying not to show that anything was wrong.

He had never thought twice about their easy touching before, despite the occasional wild rumors concerning their orientation floating around the department. The rumors were just jealousy talking -- sour grapes, and Valenti never worried about it.

After all, he and O'Brian dated different women nearly every night of the week, and everybody knew partners were supposed to be tight. So what if they hugged and wrestled and rough-housed a little now and then? Valenti and O'Brian had the best arrest record and fewer unsolved cases than any other team on the force. And it was obvious to anyone that, despite the physical affection between them, they were both as straight as a ruler.

So Valenti had always told himself. But now it was a struggle not to pull away when O'Brian touched him, a struggle to maintain a straight face and act like everything was normal when he felt like his heart was being ripped out over and over again.

Because as good a friend as he was, Valenti knew that Sean O'Brian could never be anything more to him than that -- just a friend...

* * *

"Hey, Nicky. Earth to Valenti..." He blinked and looked again into the concerned sea-green eyes of his partner. Turk had drifted away to the back, and they were alone at the bar.

"Huh?"

"I *said*, what should I wear to the club tonight? You sure you're okay? You're startin' to make me worried, ya know?"

"Yeah, I'm fine. Just, um..." Valenti cleared his throat and tried to drag his mind from the depressing subject of his hopeless love. "Just wear what you usually wear. It'll be fine."

"You sayin' my clothes look gay, partner?" O'Brian demanded, but there was a slight twinkle in his eye that let Valenti know he was just playing around.

"Nah, but your jeans are tight enough that nobody's gonna notice anything else." Valenti tried to joke and then wished he hadn't.

"You been watchin' my ass, Valenti?" O'Brian grinned at him and stood up from his stool to pull up the hem of his leather jacket and reveal the body part in question. Valenti was glad the ShySide was nearly deserted, but even so, there were a few strange looks thrown their way.

"Hey, get that outta my face. Save it for the club tonight, will you?" Valenti complained, putting out a hand to keep his partner at bay. Unfortunately it landed right on the round, tight ass in front of him, and O'Brian backed into the touch, purring like a cat.

"Mmm, nice, Nicky. Grabbin' a handful before we even get to the RamJack, huh?"

"Keep your voice down!" Valenti hissed, pulling back his hand as though he'd been burned. Now there were several dark glares pointed in their direction since the regular patrons of the ShySide weren't exactly up for a walk on the wild side. "This isn't the time or the place to act like that, Sean."

"Just gettin' into character, Nick," his partner said mildly. "You never used to care when we joked around. What's eatin' you lately?"

"Well, just save your character for the club tonight," Valenti returned, not answering the question. But his heart sank a little lower as he realized he would have to try harder to act normal around O'Brian. Because what had gotten into him was love, and he could never, ever risk letting his partner know.

Chapter Four

Antwon -- or Twonnie, as they were instructed to call him -- wasn't exactly what Valenti had expected. He was a slender young man with milk-chocolate skin and wide, liquid brown eyes that Valenti suspected of being enhanced with mascara, but that was as far as the make-up went. Valenti was relieved by that; he had been expecting someone flagrantly flamboyant -- maybe even a drag queen. But Turk's cousin was dressed more conservatively than their friend and informant usually was, or at least the color scheme of his clothes was quieter.

He was wearing a tight pair of ragged cut-off shorts that hugged his slim hips, and a too small, too tight black T-shirt, which ended just below his nipples. Valenti couldn't help comparing the shorts with a pair O'Brian sometimes jogged in when he could nag his partner into jogging with him.

"That's quite an outfit you got there, Twonnie," O'Brian said affably as they settled into the seats around a rickety table. Turk's cousin had saved it for them, and it sat to one side of the crowded dance floor. "I Will Survive" thrummed though the sound system, and the disco ball threw innumerable tiny flecks of light over everything as couples swayed to the beat all around them in the crowded darkness. Only, most of the couples were men, Valenti realized uneasily. Dancing close…touching each other…

"You like?" Turk's cousin stood up and performed an impromptu twirl before seating himself and crossing his legs daintily.

"Yeah," O'Brian said without a touch of irony. "In fact, Valenti and I were thinkin' about getting' something like that for ourselves."

"What, *both* of you?" Twonnie raised one delicate eyebrow disapprovingly.

"Well, yeah. Look, Turk *did* tell you what we're doing, right?" O'Brian frowned and put one hand on Valenti's shoulder. "We're gonna go undercover at the RamJack, so we need any information you can give us. Plus a few wardrobe hints, if you don't mind."

"Oh, I don't mind. But, honey, if you both go into the RamJack dressed like I am tonight, you'll be eaten alive. Might as well throw a piece of raw meat into a cage full of hungry tigers." He shivered theatrically and shook his head. "You wouldn't stand a chance."

"Well, then, how are we supposed to dress?" Valenti spoke up for the first time, trying to keep his eyes off the male couples all around them and ignore the warmth of his partner's hand on his arm. *What would it be like to dance with O'Brian that way*, he wondered. To hold him close...

"Well, let me see...stand up."

Shrugging at each other, the two men complied with the request, turning slowly in place before sitting back down. Twonnie nodded his head as though satisfied with himself.

"You," he pointed at Valenti, "get to be the daddy."

"The what?" Valenti wondered what the hell Twonnie was talking about.

"The sugar-daddy, honey. Everybody in the scene knows the RamJack is where all the wealthy sugar-daddies take their boy toys for fun in the sun. None of the twinkies can get in without a well-to-do sponsor, if you know what I mean."

"So I guess that makes me the boy toy." O'Brian's voice was mild, but his face was dark, and his eyes flashed emerald with irritation.

"'Fraid so, sweetie." Twonnie seemed not the least bit fazed by O'Brian's anger.

"Why?" O'Brian asked the same thing Valenti was wondering. "Why does Valenti get to be the 'daddy' and I have to play the twinkie? We're almost exactly the same age."

"Age doesn't have anything to do with this relationship, honey. We're talking money and *dominance*. Specifically, the daddy has both and the boy has neither. And as for why your partner gets to be the daddy, several reasons." Twonnie ticked them off on slim brown fingers that had, Valenti noticed, an impeccable manicure.

"First of all, Mr. Tall, Dark, and Handsome is just that -- *tall*. He has broad shoulders, and he gives off those brooding, dangerous vibes like crazy. *Very* butch. Sorry, honey, but he just *looks* more like the dominant type. Also, he's got that kind of 'fuck the cost, bring me the best' look about him. An air of *privilege*, if you will. I bet he comes from money; am I right, gorgeous?" Twonnie batted his lashes and leaned across the spindly table to address Valenti, making him distinctly uncomfortable.

"I...ah, my folks had some cash," he mumbled at last, wondering if he really did look brooding and dangerous when what he mostly felt was uncomfortable. The money was one of the reasons he'd been anxious to get away from home -- the weight of it pressing down on him, demanding he do things his father's way. Putting some distance between himself and the family money had freed up his life a lot, and he wasn't anxious to go back to it.

"See?" Twonnie turned to O'Brian triumphantly, proving his point. "Your man Valenti here has had some experience with the upper crust, and he knows how to act it. Whereas you, honey...well, don't take this wrong, but you've got the streets written all over you. You grew up in a rough neighborhood, didn't you? I'm thinking from your accent maybe even the mean streets of Boston. Pahk the cah in the Havahd yahd, right?"

O'Brian looked surprised. "Geez, what are you, kid -- a psychology major, or just a student of the human condition?"

"Sociology," Twonnie said primly. "There's more to this little twinkie than meets the eye, gentlemen. I'll have my master's degree in June, but that doesn't mean I don't enjoy playing the scene. Or that I mind helping you play, too, if you can put Vincent Conrad away. The boy that OD'd last week was my good friend."

His eyes glimmered gently in the gloom of the club, and for a moment Valenti was afraid their guide to the gay world was going to burst into tears. Apparently O'Brian feared the same thing because he reached out and put a comforting hand on one of Twonnie's slender shoulders.

Valenti was surprised at the bitter zing of jealousy that shot through him to see his partner's square, well-shaped hand resting on someone else's shoulder. *Get a grip on yourself; he's just being a nice guy. Just doing what he always does for you.* The thought wasn't the least bit comforting.

To distract himself, Valenti heard himself saying, "So, we've established that I'm more manly so I get to play the 'daddy,' but what, ah, *qualities* does my lovely partner here have that make him so fitting to play the 'boy'?"

"Don't kid yourself, honey," Twonnie said flatly, raising an immaculately groomed eyebrow at him. "Submitting doesn't make you less of a man. In fact, it takes a hell of a lot more guts to take it than to dish it out, *if* you know what I mean."

"Not really," O'Brian murmured, giving Valenti a sardonic look from the corner of his eye.

"That's right, and you better hope you don't find out the hard way, *stud*." Twonnie actually leaned across the table and poked O'Brian in the chest. "The RamJack can be a rough place if you wander into the wrong area. You want to keep your cherry, you better stay out of the Dark Knight and the Minotaur's Lair."

"The what and the where?" O'Brian looked as confused as Valenti felt.

"That's just two of the areas you want to avoid if you want to keep your virginity, honey." Twonnie smiled a little at their obvious discomfort. "I'd make you a list of all the rest, but there's too many to go into. In fact, it's really not safe for a couple of straights like you two to go to the RamJack at all. Too bad they couldn't find some gay cops to do this bit. If Conrad figures out you two are not who you say you are, you'll be in a world of hurt."

O'Brian cleared his throat. "There are no out gay cops, Twonnie. Out to each other, maybe, but not out to the brass or their brothers in blue. You oughta know that, if you have any friends in the 'scene' that are in the department. Valenti and I were picked because we've been together a long time -- we're comfortable together." He put his hand on Valenti's arm again and squeezed.

"Comfortable, hmm?" Twonnie regarded them skeptically and then nodded slowly. "Well, I can see that, I guess. At least you're not sitting there all stiff and straight and afraid to touch each other. But in order to pull this off, your body language has got to be even more loose and natural than it already is. You need to be touching each other *all the time*."

"But we do -- at least, most of the time," O'Brian protested.

Valenti nodded, thinking how he used to take the easy touching between them for granted. That was before O'Brian's hand on his arm sent a tingling fire straight to his crotch. He crossed his legs uncomfortably and wished O'Brian would take his hand away, but he couldn't possibly say so.

"No, no -- not all this manly we-are-brothers-let-me-pat-you-on-the-shoulder shit. Pardon my French, honey. Detective Valenti --" He turned earnestly to Valenti. "-- *you* have to touch possessively -- put your hands on your boy with *authority* so everybody gets the message he's yours. Otherwise, he's up for grabs, and you don't want that at the RamJack.

"Now, you --" Twonnie turned to O'Brian, who was watching him intently, his hand still on Valenti's arm. "You need to work on acting like his boy. It helps that you're blond and cute, and you should definitely work that as much as possible. And use your playful side, if you've got one, stud -- joke and tease a lot, play up to your man. Touch him like you need reassurance -- to make sure he's still there and interested in you. Kiss the side of his neck, sit between his legs, put your head on his shoulder -- remind him you're his one and only. Am I making myself clear?"

"Perfectly," Valenti said miserably. It was almost like Twonnie was inside his head, making a list of all the things he wished he could do with his partner but could never dare. He couldn't believe O'Brian wasn't raising holy hell about some of Twonnie's "suggestions," but his partner just nodded, a thoughtful look in his green eyes.

"And can you do it? Because if you have any doubts, you'd better back out now. The RamJack is no place to play around, boys." Twonnie looked so serious that Valenti almost turned to his partner and suggested that they do just that. Before he could say anything, O'Brian growled, "Valenti and me don't back out of anything. We're playin' for keeps here, and we'll do what it takes."

Twonnie shook his head, a sorrowful look in his liquid brown eyes. "I hope you know what you're saying, honey, and I hope you can follow through with it. Once you go in those big black doors, you're in Conrad's domain, and Lord help you if he suspects you're not just another daddy and his boy out for some fun."

"What's the worst that could happen?" Valenti asked reasonably. "He won't deal with us. Right?"

"Wrong." Twonnie said flatly. He sat up straighter in his chair and tugged at the hem of his too-tight T-shirt. "I guess nobody told you this, but a couple of years back a rival drug lord sent in a couple of his lieutenants to try and shanghai Conrad. But see, they were straight, and they acted it. Conrad was on them like a duck on a June bug when he found out the truth -- which, by the way, didn't take him long. That night those two boys had a visit from some very scary leather daddies. I heard they could barely sit still on the nice plush seats of the limo Conrad sent them home in."

"Wasn't he worried about starting a war?" O'Brian asked, frowning.

"You think those two admitted what happened to them?" Twonnie demanded. "Why, that might damage their precious *manhood*. No, they just told their boss Conrad was on to them and they were sent back as a message -- next time, somebody dies. Nobody's tried anything hinky with Master Conrad since. Word gets around, honey. *Believe* me, it does."

"So you're sayin' if Valenti and I don't act the part, we could be in deep shit," O'Brian said bluntly.

"That's putting it mildly, sweetie," Twonnie said. "And from what Turk said, you've only got a week to practice your act, so you better get to it." He gestured at both of them.

"What, right now?" Valenti asked, feeling slightly panicked.

"What do you want us to do, kiss?" O'Brian asked, a lot more coolly than Valenti would have believed possible. What had gotten into his partner lately? Valenti would have bet even money that if someone had suggested that Sean O'Brian was willing to kiss another man -- even his partner and best friend -- O'Brian would have punched the chump in the mouth. But now here he was suggesting it himself.

Twonnie looked amused. "No, honey," he told O'Brian. "You'll have to work up to that, I think. But why don't you take tall, dark, and beautiful here out for a spin on the dance floor?"

"What, *here?*" Valenti asked, knowing that he sounded like a broken record, but unable to help himself.

"Where else did you have in mind, honey, Grand Central Station? Of course *here.* Don't get that panicked look on your face; I'm not asking you to throw your partner facedown on the table and screw him. I just said *dance.*" Twonnie looked disgusted with them. "If you can't even dance with each other, then you might as well forget it -- you may have to do a lot more than that to pass at the RamJack."

"We can do it," O'Brian said defiantly. "C'mon, Nicky, I'll even let you lead." He stood up from the rickety table and grabbed Valenti's hand, pulling him reluctantly to his feet.

"Now try to blend in -- as much as you can in those clothes, anyway," Twonnie instructed with a sniff, clearly disapproving of their plain jeans and T-shirts. "Watch the other couples around you and just play follow the leader. But if they lead you into the men's room -- watch out!" He giggled at his own joke and made shooing motions at the pair of them. "Go on, I'll watch from here and give you a full critique when you get back."

"C'mon, Nick," O'Brian said again, pulling him toward the dance floor. Valenti realized that his partner was still holding his hand and that their fingers were entwined. It was the way you held hands with your lover, not your best friend.

"Okay," he said stupidly, stumbling along behind O'Brian, who was always so graceful.

Once out on the dance floor, it wasn't so bad. "Disco Inferno" was playing, and O'Brian dropped his hand to dance to the lively beat. Valenti had nothing to do but admire his partner's lithe gyrations and try to copy them. Although he wasn't nearly the dancer O'Brian was, he thought he wasn't half bad, and he was even beginning to enjoy himself a little until the music changed.

"Here's something for all you lovers on the floor tonight," the DJ announced, and something soft and romantic began playing. Valenti looked around him; everywhere, men were holding each other in pairs, swaying gently to the slow beat. Some were making out right on the dimly lit dance floor. Valenti tried to keep from imagining doing that with his partner, but he kept seeing himself taking that beloved face in his hands and leaning closer and closer until he could taste those soft lips. He was about to bolt back to the table when he felt O'Brian's hand on his arm, and then he was being pulled into a warm embrace.

"C'mon, babe, dance with me," O'Brian whispered in his ear, and then they were dancing, touching in a way they had never touched before, swaying to the music chest to chest and crotch to crotch. Valenti felt like his universe was turning inside out. He and his best friend had always been close, but he'd never dreamed they'd ever be close enough for O'Brian to feel comfortable slow dancing with him. But even though it was utterly bizarre, it was also typical O'Brian -- his partner never did anything halfway.

Valenti found his arms were around O'Brian's shoulders and O'Brian's arms were around his waist, and somehow it was the most natural feeling in the world. His face was buried in the thick, red-blond hair, and the clean, male musk of his partner was making him feel almost drunk. He was hard as a rock, and he knew O'Brian had to feel it, but if he did, he didn't try to move away or say anything about it. Then he realized that his partner was hard, too. He could feel it clearly through those skin-tight jeans, a lump the size of a Coke bottle rubbing against his crotch with a delicious friction that made him dizzy with want and need.

Why was O'Brian hard? Valenti wondered about it as well as his lust-fogged brain would let him. He knew for certain that it had nothing to do with O'Brian dancing close to him; the man just didn't swing that way. Period. His friend was probably just hard from the buzz of dancing to the fast music earlier, Valenti finally decided. He knew, because it was fairly obvious in the tight pants O'Brian always wore, that his partner often got aroused during times of excitement -- during a bust or before a big date. Or when they went out dancing with girls -- this was the first time they'd gone dancing together, of course.

"Killing me softly..." Roberta Flack crooned, and Valenti thought fuzzily, *That's exactly what he's doing. Killing me, man -- I can't take much more of this...* That was when he felt the soft, warm brush of lips against the side of his neck.

"Wha--?" he started to say, pulling back from his partner, but O'Brian shushed him.

"Just practicing, like the man said. Don't look so surprised, Valenti; he's watchin' us. He doesn't think we can do it -- let's prove him wrong." O'Brian smiled at him in the smoky gloom of the club, and Valenti's heart sank even though he knew it was irrational to be disappointed. It was just O'Brian's competitive nature coming out again, not anything special between them. He should have known -- trust his partner to get competitive about anything, even how well they could play gay. If Twonnie said they couldn't, then O'Brian was determined to prove they could, simple as that.

"All right, you just scared me is all," he said, reluctantly allowing himself to be pulled into his partner's arms again. "Didn't expect it."

"Well, you should've," O'Brian complained. "He *did* say to kiss your neck. And that's a lot less than half these guys are doin'." He nodded to the couples all around them and adjusted his stance so that he fit more snugly against Valenti's body as though to prove his point. Valenti noticed that his partner's hard-on hadn't gone down a bit, although his own had decreased considerably.

"I'm not complaining. I'm just saying give a guy some warning before you start that. I'm not exactly used to it, you know," he answered, settling his arms around his partner and burying his face in the thatch of blond hair again.

"Consider yourself warned then, babe," O'Brian whispered in his ear, and then Valenti felt it again, that soft, gentle brush against his neck -- the tentative touch of his partner's mouth on his throat.

"You smell good, Sean," he muttered, having no idea what he was saying. His words seemed to make his partner bolder, because after a moment Valenti felt another kiss, this one stronger and more certain. Then O'Brian's mouth, hot and deliciously right, was open against his throat and his partner was not just kissing but licking and sucking, drawing a groan from Valenti's lips.

It didn't matter anymore to him that this was just O'Brian's competitive nature coming out. The physical stimulation was too strong to deny, and Valenti felt his cock grow rock hard and solid, throbbing in the denim prison of his jeans as his partner explored his neck with his warm, sensual lips.

"You taste good," O'Brian murmured, at last pulling back to lay his head on Valenti's shoulder. "Kinda salty…"

"You think?" he murmured back. "Go figure -- must be my aftershave."

"What're you wearing?" O'Brian asked, nuzzling against Valenti's chest.

"English Leather," Valenti whispered back. He felt O'Brian twitch in his arms, and then there was a subdued snort of laughter.

"My men wear English Leather, or they don't wear anything at all," his partner quoted in a strangled voice. Suddenly the tension between them broke and they were holding each other and laughing until they got dirty looks from the other couples on the floor.

"C'mon, Valenti. We better go before they kick us out." O'Brian towed him by the hand back to the rickety table where Twonnie was waiting.

"That was excellent right up until the last," Twonnie said, steepling his slim brown fingers and staring at them both intently. "I don't know what cracked you up, but try not to let it happen at the RamJack."

"Check." O'Brian was still laughing, although not as maniacally as before. "Better pack a different aftershave, Nicky."

"Check." Valenti was still laughing right along with him. *If we can still cut up together, maybe everything will be okay*, he thought, enjoying the sensation of being at ease around his partner again. *Maybe these feelings I'm having for him are just some crazy phase I'm going through and it'll all work out in the end...*

His hopes lasted until the next morning at work at the Metro precinct.

* * *

"Hey, buddy, must've had a hot date last night, huh?" Johnson smirked at him, and Valenti frowned and put down the stack of paperwork he'd been trying to get through.

"Why does everybody keep asking me that?" he demanded. "You're the fourth person who's made some kind of smart-ass comment to me today. I don't get it."

"Well, maybe it has something to do with the huge hickey on the side of your neck, lover boy." Maria from Records grinned at him. "Who are you dating, a vampire?" She leaned over his desk and ran a finger playfully down the left side of Valenti's neck. *The side O'Brian kissed me on last night,* he realized. *Last night...oh, my God...*

"Hey, Valenti, how ya doin'?" It was his partner right behind him. Valenti rose from the desk and grabbed O'Brian's arm, towing him toward the men's room. "Hey, what gives?" his partner protested, but Valenti didn't say a thing until he'd gotten them both safely into the room and checked to make sure there was no one in any of the stalls.

"Look at my neck," he demanded in a low voice, after glancing briefly at it in the mirror. Sure enough, there was an enormous hickey, a dark, purplish-red spot right under the big pulse point beneath his ear. He must have missed it that morning because he hadn't had time to shave -- no wonder everyone was asking if he'd gotten lucky! O'Brian looked puzzled, but he glanced obligingly at the spot his partner was pointing to.

"Hey," he said admiringly. "You get some action last night after we went home?"

"No, I went home and went to bed. *You* did this to me," Valenti hissed fiercely, turning back to the mirror again. He hadn't had a hickey this size since the night of his senior prom, when he'd gotten lucky with Ginger Foster. "What were you thinking?" he asked his partner. "What were you trying to do -- mark me or something?"

"Or something," O'Brian agreed. "Look, Valenti, I'm sorry. I didn't realize you'd mark so easy; you're not exactly the pale, easy-to-bruise type. I didn't do it on purpose, honest. I just...well, I guess I got carried away. Tryin' to prove we could act the part, ya know?" he added quickly, perhaps seeing the incredulous lift of his partner's eyebrows.

"Damn right you got carried away." Valenti frowned sternly, but it was impossible to stay angry with O'Brian for long, especially when he got that hang-dog look on his face. Also, he couldn't help thinking about the way he'd gotten the hickey --

O'Brian's crotch rubbing against his, those warm hands on his back, that hot mouth on his neck... To his horror, Valenti found he was getting a hard-on just thinking about it. He crouched closer to the mirror, hoping his partner wouldn't notice.

"Look, I know things got kinda weird last night, and I feel like it was my fault, so I apologize," O'Brian continued. "I feel like I'm pushin' you into this thing and you don't really want to go. I mean, if it weirds you out that much, we can drop it, Nick. I want this case, but it's not more important to me than our partnership -- than our friendship, understand?" His voice was disappointed but firm, as though he expected Valenti to jump at the chance to get out of the assignment. But his body language was tense with longing.

"I know," Valenti muttered. He looked at his partner bouncing on the balls of his feet in the cool tile sterility of the men's room, and knew that, for whatever reason, O'Brian really *wanted* this case. It was the first big one they'd been offered since his partner had been nearly killed by a trip-wired junkie strung out on PCP in the dirty back alley of the Chinese restaurant they had decided to try that fateful night six months ago. O'Brian had been stabbed multiple times before Valenti could get to him.

Valenti still had nightmares about it -- about blood, so red it looked black, gushing out between his fingers onto the filthy pavement as he begged O'Brian to hold on, partner, help is coming, just *hold on.* It was so good to see his partner back on top of his game. O'Brian's recovery from the vicious wounds had been long and painful, and now that he was in top form again, Valenti knew his usually active partner was tired of being desk-bound and was itching for action.

O'Brian had a natural athleticism, an energy that made his every move graceful. Valenti had often thought his partner was like a leopard, full of lithe, barely contained power waiting to explode into action. And despite everything that could go wrong and everything that had already gone wrong, Valenti found he didn't have the heart to deny him. *God help me if he ever asks for something I can't give.* He sighed deeply and ran a tanned hand through his black hair. "Nah, it's all right," he said at last, heavily. "Let's just try to take it easy, okay?"

"Okay," O'Brian agreed affably. "C'mon, partner, let's go tell everybody how you got that hickey having a three-way with Whatzername and her sister last night."

Valenti burst out laughing -- he couldn't help it. And he thought again that if they could just stay comfortable around each other, keep breaking the tension with laughter and jokes, that everything might be okay.

But the RamJack, as Twonnie had tried to warn them, was no laughing matter.

Chapter Five

A loud pounding on the door of the suite brought Valenti out of his reverie. Glancing at his watch, he realized he'd been sitting on the side of the vast bed for almost forty-five minutes, just thinking. The pounding came again, louder this time, and he jumped up and went for the door.

"Coming!" He pulled back the solid oak door to find a sheepish-looking O'Brian flanked by a pair of the biggest goons he'd ever laid eyes on. One had black hair, and the other was blond; both were built like gorillas and dressed from head to foot entirely in black leather. The blond-haired goon had a face like a side of beef, and one burly hand was clutching O'Brian's bicep in a death grip.

Before he remembered the wealthy sugar-daddy role he was supposed to be playing, Valenti blurted out, "O'Brian, you okay?" Then, seeing the eyes of the black-haired goon narrow, he quickly added, "What's this about?"

"Is this your boy, Mr. Valenti?" the goon on the left demanded, shaking O'Brian by the arm the way a big dog might shake a little one. They had decided to keep their names as close as possible to the real thing, to avoid confusion.

Valenti saw the belligerent look in his partner's eye and answered quickly. "Yes, he's mine. Is there a problem?" He almost added "officer" before he thought about it. The two goons had the menacing air of authority that branded them as part of the RamJack's security force.

"He was found wandering in an unsecured area without his sponsor," goon number one replied, shaking O'Brian again to make his point. The action aroused possessive feelings in Valenti he had never felt before.

"Is that a problem?" he snapped, reaching out to take O'Brian's arm himself and pulling the shorter man toward him. Without thinking, he looped a proprietary arm around his partner's neck. He felt O'Brian stiffen for a moment, and then his partner's arms went around his waist and the compact body melted naturally against his side. *Good for you, Sean -- play along,* he thought absently as he continued to give his iciest glare to the two gorillas at the door.

"It can be," the blond goon said. "Unless you wish your boy to be available to other members of the club…"

"Absolutely not! O'Br-- Sean is *mine.*" Valenti cursed himself for nearly slipping on the name again, and he didn't miss the disbelieving look both goons were giving him, either. Damn it, he was playing this badly; he'd never been so rattled while undercover before. What was wrong with him? Trying to regain control of the situation, he stood up straighter and said, "Sean is my exclusive property. I would be very upset if anyone else…" He couldn't think quite how to end it, so he said again, "He's mine."

"Then you'd better keep him close, Mr. *Valenti,*" the black-haired goon growled, speaking for the first time. He had a voice like someone gargling with gravel. "An unaccompanied boy is free game at the RamJack. If you want to keep his tight ass all to yourself, you'd better keep an eye on *Sean* here." The emphasis he put on the names let Valenti know that neither goon believed they were who they said they were. A bad start, even if they were only assuming he was a closeted gay trying to protect his identity by using a false name.

"I'll try to remember that. Now, if you'll excuse me, gentlemen..." Valenti used his free arm, the one that wasn't looped around his partner's neck, to swing the door shut in their beefy faces. After a moment, the muffled sound of heavy footsteps on thick carpet could be heard, and he sighed in relief and turned to his partner.

"Hey, don't look at me -- how was I s'posed to know?" O'Brian shrugged Valenti's arm off his shoulders, frowning. "I was just checkin' out the scene. I saw a dark area -- looked perfect for drug deals. So I decided to check it out."

"See any *dealing* going on, partner?" Valenti asked, crossing his arms over his chest. He was half amused and half dismayed to see the slow, red flush creeping into his partner's throat and cheeks. When was the last time anything had made O'Brian blush? Valenti couldn't remember.

"Not...ah...not the kind of deals I was lookin' for," his partner admitted, scowling. "Just..." He cleared his throat. "Just a bunch of guys doin'...a bunch of stuff."

"Doing each other" is probably more like it. But Valenti didn't say it out loud. He sighed and went over to sit on the bed. "Well, did you find anything out at all before those lugs caught you wandering around 'without a sponsor'?"

"I cased the joint pretty well, actually." O'Brian grinned at him and sauntered over to lean against one of the elaborately carved bedposts, crossing his arms over his chest. "As Turk would say, it's op-u-*lent.* They got an Olympic-sized swimming pool, Jacuzzi, steam room, dining hall, pool room, library, and several lounges -- don't think I saw all of them. It's like a regular city in here -- completely self contained. But, Valenti, you know the weirdest thing?"

"What's that?"

"No women *anywhere*." O'Brian shook his head at the abysmal lack. "I didn't even see any in the kitchen or dining area. This whole resort is male only -- even the maids are guys. I tell ya, it's weird."

"Weird..." Valenti echoed. He wasn't surprised that O'Brian had an eye out for girls and was disappointed at not finding any. His partner had always been a ladies' man. "It's probably a good thing," he pointed out. "You start putting the make on some hottie, even if she was just the help, it would blow a big hole in our cover."

O'Brian looked offended. "Hey, give me some credit, Nick; I know what we're here for." O'Brian sidled over to the side of the bed and sat by his partner, brushing Valenti's thigh with his own. "I know I'm supposed to be your exclusive property." His hand drifted to Valenti's knee and gave it a provocative squeeze. The warmth of his palm seemed to go straight to Valenti's groin.

"Cut it out." Valenti pushed his partner's hand off his knee impatiently, angry at O'Brian's use of his own hasty words and his body's reaction to the other man's touch. "Quit clowning around, would you? This is serious business."

"Hey, I *am* being serious," his partner protested, getting angry in turn. "I'm tryin' to keep in character here, Valenti. Remember what Twonnie said -- if they don't buy our act, then we're screwed. Maybe *literally*. And I don't think either one of us was doing a very good job selling to thing one and thing two at the door there." He nodded at the solid oak door and frowned.

"I know I wasn't very smooth back there." Valenti shook his head, feeling defeated. "It's this whole situation, Sean -- it's just got me rattled. I hardly know how to act..."

"Don't worry about it, partner. Just follow my lead." O'Brian patted him on the knee again, and this time Valenti didn't push his partner's hand away. He wondered why O'Brian felt so damn confident acting like they were in a gay relationship, while he himself could barely manage. He was basically being given a chance to act exactly the way he wished he could toward his partner, and he was blowing it big time; whereas O'Brian was coming across as the perfect gay twinkie. Probably because Valenti was too emotionally invested, and to O'Brian, it was all just an act. Just another undercover assignment.

"I don't know, O'Brian. What if we have to...do things?" It was something he had avoided talking about in the week preceding the assignment, but now Valenti felt it couldn't be ignored any longer. Despite Twonnie's warning, he had managed to make himself believe that he and O'Brian would be able to get away with just standing close to each other and looking possessive. Now that they were actually inside the RamJack, behind its forbidding black doors, he found that he couldn't so easily fool himself.

"What if we have to...I don't know...kiss each other?" he asked, feeling as awkward as a teenager on his first date. Surely his partner would deny the likelihood of such a scenario and tell him not to be silly. But O'Brian surprised him again.

"We'll do it," O'Brian said calmly. "We'll do whatever it takes to nail this bastard Conrad." He turned and gave his partner a quick kiss on the cheek as if to prove his point. "See, that's not so bad, is it?"

"That's not the kind of kiss I'm worried about," Valenti muttered, reaching up to touch the place on his cheek O'Brian had kissed. It tingled, and his whole face felt hot, as though he'd been branded. He reflected that maybe he should get over his shock at O'Brian's apparent change of heart and just accept his partner's willingness to do anything it took to get this particular job done.

"You shouldn't be worried about *any* kind of kiss, Valenti," O'Brian insisted. "Look, we just have to get over this whole...physical thing and concentrate on what's really important -- busting Conrad. Everything else had to take a back seat to that, ya know? So if you have to kiss me or grab my ass or whatever you have to do out there, just do it already and don't worry about it. We both know it's all just part of the act. Okay?"

"Okay." Valenti shrugged dubiously and tried not to think about it. "So, what now?"

"Now we get ready for dinner, and I hope you brought your tux because I think it's s'posed to be a formal affair. For you, anyway. I just get to dress like the twinkie I am." O'Brian grinned at him and hopped off the bed. "C'mon, babe, let's get you lookin' beautiful."

Chapter Six

"That's him -- gotta be," O'Brian whispered in his ear, while pretending to kiss him on the neck.

Valenti felt the soft brush of lips against his throat as his partner spoke; apparently O'Brian wasn't taking any chances on faking the affectionate gesture. Deciding to follow his partner's lead, he cupped the back of O'Brian's neck and whispered back, "That's him, all right." He finished the sentence with a soft kiss on his partner's cheek and pulled back, but not too far.

They were seated with about thirty other "daddies" and "boys" around a huge rectangular table that reminded Valenti too much of his childhood for comfort. He could remember vividly the long, boring dinner parties his parents had thrown, where a young Nicholas was expected to be on his best behavior at all times. He supposed he should be grateful for that experience now; it was amazing how quickly all the proper etiquette and table manners came back. He had been quietly instructing O'Brian on which fork to use for the first course, when his partner had leaned in and whispered the information about Conrad.

O'Brian was still casting glances toward the head of the table, and Valenti risked a quick look as well. They were seated around the middle of the table, close enough to study the man in question without making conversation with him, much to Valenti's relief. Vincent Conrad was tall -- taller than Valenti -- and as lean as a greyhound. He had lank, medium-length, brownish-black hair that framed a thin face with a nose as sharp as a knife and cool gray eyes that skimmed over the table dispassionately. Valenti took one look at those eyes and thought, *shark*.

Hovering by Conrad's shoulder was a small, slim Hispanic man with large brown eyes and hair the color of licorice -- so black it had blue highlights. The man -- or "boy," for Valenti supposed that must be his designation -- was probably in his early twenties, and he was dressed in the too-tight jean shorts and white tank top that seemed to be the unofficial uniform for all twinkies at the RamJack.

Of course, O'Brian had felt the need to go one better; in addition to shorts that were so tight Valenti was surprised his partner could even breathe in them, O'Brian was also wearing a tight black tank top with the words "Boy Toy" written on the front in hot-pink cursive script. When he'd put it on, Valenti had simply shaken his head.

"What, you don't like?" O'Brian had had that twinkle in his eye that meant he was teasing his partner and loving every minute of it.

"Where did you even *get* that?" Valenti had asked, not sure whether to be annoyed or amused. He decided to settle for halfway in between. He himself was dressed in an expensive, conservative black suit and a gold tie that picked up the golden flecks in his brown eyes. It felt strange to be wearing something so unlike his usual casual undercover street clothes, but he considered that his partner must feel even stranger in his get-up -- although you would never know it, the way O'Brian strutted.

"Got it from Twonnie." His partner had grinned proudly. "'S what all the well-dressed twinkies are wearin' this season." Valenti found he didn't have an answer for that, and so they had made their way to the dining hall, studying the other daddies and boys around them as they went.

Twonnie had been right; age was definitely not the sole criteria for designation of class at the RamJack. Although several of the well-dressed men seated around them were older, there were many middle-aged and young men scattered around the table. The twinkies, however, usually were younger than their "sponsors," although Valenti noted a few who seemed to be around the same age, like he and O'Brian. He wondered briefly if they were lovers just there to play some kind of twisted dominance game.

Because dominance was definitely the order of the day. All around the table, the twinkies cuddled close to their respective sponsors or pouted and flirted with others. Whatever they said or did, it was obviously aimed at the well-dressed men they were with -- the men with the power. *That's me*, Valenti thought. He had a vague idea he ought to be treating O'Brian more aggressively, touching him more possessively, as Twonnie had recommended, but he didn't really know how to begin. His partner, however, seemed to have no problem getting into character.

"Look, he's mad at his twink," O'Brian murmured in his ear, kissing him again and directing Valenti's attention to the head of the table once more. Sure enough, Conrad was speaking in an angry half-whisper to the small man by his side, and Valenti could catch a few words of the conversation even from where he was sitting.

"Your attitude leaves much to be desired, Julio. I do not care for the way you are acting tonight," Conrad was saying in a severe tone. He had a slightly foreign accent Valenti couldn't quite place. The boy frowned and slid one slim brown hand over his tight ass provocatively. Unlike his sponsor, he didn't bother to lower his voice.

"Well, maybe I should find someone who does then, *Master*," he said sarcastically, scanning the table for other prospects. Happening to catch Valenti's eye, he threw a blindingly white grin in his direction. Uncertain of what to do, Valenti smiled back warily; he had never been cruised so openly before, at least not by a man.

"You see?" Julio's voice was loud enough for everyone at the table to hear now. "That fine gentleman over there seems to like me, attitude or not." He started to glide around the table to make Valenti's better acquaintance. Valenti was just wondering how the hell he was supposed to handle this situation, when it suddenly got more complicated.

As Julio was closing the gap between them, Conrad's long arm shot out, and he grabbed his boy by the wrist in a grip that looked like it could crush bone. "Not so fast, *mi mariposa*," he growled and pulled the hapless Julio in for a kiss that looked more like oral rape.

Bending the slim wrist until Julio whimpered pitifully and sank to the ground beside his Master's chair, Conrad leaned over and took the smaller man's mouth with a ferocity that startled Valenti. His cop's instincts always attuned to the pain of others, he'd almost risen out of the chair to help Julio when strong arms restrained him.

"Relax, babe; it's just a game they're playing," O'Brian breathed in his ear, and Valenti realized his partner was nearly sitting on his lap, having abandoned his own chair when things got tense.

"But it looks like Conrad's hurting him," he protested, keeping enough presence of mind to cover his words with a nuzzle against O'Brian's sleek, tanned throat. He could smell male musk and fresh, clean sweat and realized his partner was as nervous as he was. Somehow that made him feel a little better about the whole situation.

"Look again, Valenti -- the kid's lovin' every minute of it," O'Brian whispered while kissing his way leisurely along his partner's ear.

"What was that Conrad called him?" Valenti asked, trying not to notice the effect his partner's mouth was having on him. He felt, as always, linguistically inadequate whenever Spanish was being spoken.

"Mi mariposa means...think it means 'my little butter-fly,' somethin' like that." O'Brian continued to kiss him, and the touch of his warm lips on the sensitive ear was very distracting. When his partner started sucking his earlobe, Valenti began to wonder how the hell he was supposed to pay attention to anything else.

He tried to focus on the small tableau going on at the head of the table, and he could see that O'Brian was right. Julio was moaning all right -- but not in pain. Conrad had his arm pinned behind his back and was still holding him in a punishing grip, but the bulge Valenti could see in the front of the skin-tight jean shorts was enough to prove that Julio didn't really mind what was being done to him.

"See?" O'Brian breathed, tonguing his ear until Valenti could feel his own hard-on pushing for escape. His partner's tight ass rubbing against his crotch wasn't helping matters, either.

"Would you cut that out? You're driving me insane," he whispered, trying to push his partner off his lap in the most unobtrusive way he could. But it was clear O'Brian didn't want to be pushed away. He clung for a moment more, his arms locked around Valenti's neck, until he finally allowed himself to be removed to his own seat, where he pouted every bit as convincingly as Julio had been doing.

"Are you going to behave from now on?" Valenti heard Conrad growl as he watched the scene at the front of the table play out.

"Yes, Master." Julio's voice was breathy now, his eyes bright and his full mouth swollen from the punishing kisses he had just received. But he looked just as happy as a pig in shit, as O'Brian might have said.

Valenti couldn't help wondering what it would be like to take his partner's mouth like that, to hold O'Brian down and kiss him until he couldn't breathe. Or to be held down himself. Again he felt his cock throb in his pants.

Am I going to spend every minute we're here in a constant state of arousal? Valenti wondered in dismay. *Better jerk off when I go to bed tonight.* Then he remembered that he and O'Brian were going to be sleeping in the same bed, and he nearly groaned -- no relief in sight. At the head of the table, Conrad and his boy were wrapping up their little performance.

"To whom do you belong?" Conrad asked, running one lean finger along the side of his boy toy's brown cheek.

"You, Master. Only and always to you," Julio whispered, and Valenti could tell he meant it. Unlike the cool gray shark-eyes Conrad had fixed on him, the twinkie's were full of love and adoration. *He's just playing with the boy -- but the boy thinks it's the real thing*, Valenti realized. Julio was going to be in for a nasty shock if Conrad ever got tired of him.

"Go upstairs and wait for me," Conrad ordered. "I expect to find you naked in my bed, on your hands and knees, ready to be fucked when I arrive. Do you understand?"

"Yes, Master," Julio breathed, and Valenti realized this was what the boy had been angling for all along -- punishment. Should he be treating O'Brian the same way Conrad was treating Julio? He had no clue. The image of his partner naked, on his hands and knees in the middle of that vast expanse of mattress in their suite, leaped into his mind, and Valenti suddenly had difficulty getting a deep enough breath. The lightly tanned skin rippling with tense muscles, the thick, heavy cock growing hard between his partner's spread thighs, and O'Brian's eyes, a drowning, deep sea-green looking at him -- looking back over his shoulder as he invited Valenti to touch him, to take him, to *fuck* him... *No* -- he *had* to stop thinking like this. Had to concentrate on the situation at hand

and the goal of bringing Conrad to justice, as O'Brian had said. Still, that image of his partner wouldn't leave his head.

"Well, show's over for now." The voice to his left startled Valenti, and he turned to find a well-dressed gentleman with thinning reddish hair and round glasses, who was probably ten or fifteen years older than Valenti, speaking to him.

"I'm sorry?" he said uncertainly. "Show?"

"Yes, it's the same thing every night. Julio flounces in pitching attitude, and Conrad has to discipline him. Frankly, I think Conrad's getting a little tired of it -- his twink had better cool it a little, or he'll find his tight ass out on the street, where Conrad got him in the first place. There's no shortage of tight asses in this place, as I'm sure you've noticed." The man grinned genially and raised a fluted wineglass to his lips.

"Oh, uh, yes. Yes, of course," Valenti said, remembering his role. Although the only tight ass he had been noticing lately was his partner's.

"But let me introduce myself, at least, before we start gossiping. I'm just an old queen, and you know how we queens love to dish the dirt." The man smiled again, this time almost flirtatiously, and held out a pale hand for Valenti to shake. Valenti took it, noticing how soft the palm was. "I'm Paul McGillis. Pleased to meet you. My." He winced slightly. "That's quite a grip you have there."

"Sorry." Valenti loosed his hand immediately. "Didn't mean to. The name's Valenti -- Charles Valenti."

"Well, Mr. Valenti -- or may I call you Charles?" Valenti nodded, and the man continued. "Charles, then, and please call me Paul. It's a pleasure to make your acquaintance. Am I correct in assuming this is your first time at the RamJack?"

"Well, yes," Valenti replied evasively. "I...uh...only recently heard about it, and I thought I'd try it out."

"First time out of the closet, hmm?" The reddish eyebrows rose inquisitively above the mild blue eyes, and for some absurd reason Valenti found he was blushing.

"It's that obvious, huh?" he asked, deciding he'd better play along.

"Oh, yes, I'm afraid so. But let me be the first to welcome you -- to the RamJack and the scene."

"The scene?" Valenti asked, pretending to pick at the food in front of him and noticing that O'Brian was listening intently to the whole conversation. Good, they could compare notes later.

"Yes, the scene -- the gay lifestyle, my dear. I hope coming to the RamJack won't put you off it, though -- it's kind of an extreme place for someone who's just discovered himself. Still, some people just have to jump in with both feet."

"Discovered...?" Valenti started, but the red-haired man beside him kept talking, apparently enjoying the sound of his own voice now that he was speaking on a favorite topic.

"Discovered your *sexuality*, Charles, of course," he said. "Where are you, somewhere in your early thirties? Yes, I thought so. Now, take me -- I've known from age three that I was gay, although it took me nearly twenty years to do anything about it. I remember it so well..." The pale blue eyes behind the round glasses got misty as he related what was obviously a much-loved memory.

"I was in the Navy, of all places, taking a shower and admiring the tight ass of the yeoman second-class who was showering beside me. I was trying not to be obvious, but he noticed me noticing him all the same, and he came over to me, all naked and dripping soap..." He sighed and shook his head. By this time both Valenti and O'Brian had given up all pretense of eating and were simply listening as Paul McGillis related his story.

"Well, I thought for certain that I was going to get the shit kicked out of me, as we used to say on the *USS McCarthy* -- yes, that was actually the name of my ship; could you *die?* -- But instead of killing me, Frank -- that was his name -- just looked around to make sure we were alone in the shower, and then he dropped to his knees and swallowed me whole. It was my first ever experience, and God, was it *fine*. I'll never forget it... But pardon me." He raised an eyebrow and seemed to come back to himself a little. "I just met you, so maybe we don't know each other well enough to be trading first-time stories."

"Oh, no, please. It's...fascinating," Valenti said weakly. Now he found he was being tormented with visions of being sucked off in the shower by his partner, or, alternatively, dropping to his knees and doing the sucking himself.

He would take O'Brian's thick shaft in one hand and lightly tongue the head, tasting the slippery pre-come leaking from the slit before sucking as much of his partner's heavy cock into his mouth as he could. O'Brian would moan, the water running down his golden skin, matting the thick, curling, blondish-red hair on his chest and beading on the ripe sac hanging just below his cock. Then Valenti would feel O'Brian's hands, the strong fingers slipping into his hair and urging him on...fucking his mouth... Damn it -- was he going to translate everything he saw and heard in this twisted place to fantasies about his partner? His cock gave a throb as if to say, *You better believe it, buddy*. Valenti nearly groaned aloud.

"So you'd care to share yourself?" Paul inquired, catching him off-guard. "You see, I'm a bit of a collector of such stories. I'm an author by trade, and someday I hope to write a book. All names will be changed to protect the guilty, of course." He grinned charmingly.

"Oh, well, I'm not sure…" Valenti had no idea in hell what to say. "My first time with…with a man?" he asked, trying to buy time.

"Yes, I always find first-time stories from men who have realized their sexuality fairly late in life to be that much more interesting," Paul replied, toying with his wineglass again. "I mean, how strange that must be for you -- to wake up one day and just find yourself attracted to another man instead of a woman. To finally acknowledge those feeling about your postman, your accountant -- hell, your best friend. Although I suppose the latent tendencies must already be there to start with…"

Latent tendencies, Valenti thought despairingly. Did he have some kind of predisposition toward the gay lifestyle? Was that why he suddenly found himself drawn to his partner in a more than friendly way? *Be honest, Nicholas, in a sexual way.* And yet, he felt no attraction to any other man but O'Brian; all these other twinkies in tight shorts left him cold. Could you be gay if you only wanted one other member of the same sex?

He thought about an AA meeting he'd attended with a friend once for moral support. A man had raised his hand and pointed out that he only drank every Monday, to help him get through the start of the week. Did that make him an alcoholic, he wanted to know. The group leader's answer had been an unequivocal *yes*.

"Puddin', are you badgering this nice man?" The voice came from the other side of Paul, breaking into his thoughts, and Valenti could see a sleek, platinum-blond head peeking around Paul's neatly tailored black suit.

"Not now, Remy. I'm about to add a new first-time story to my collection." Paul McGillis gestured in irritation, but the man beside him would not give up.

"Well, aren't you even goin' to introduce us?" he asked in a lilting Southern drawl that poured over Valenti's eardrums like honey. Half standing, he leaned around Paul. He had a pointed, kittenish face dominated by huge sapphire eyes and a pouting red mouth. He looked like a waif, and the tight shorts and tank top accentuated the impression. Valenti though him easily the prettiest man in the room, a dubious distinction.

"Fine." Paul blew out an irritated breath, although Valenti thought it was just for show -- an act they performed for their own enjoyment, much as Conrad and his twink had earlier. "This shameless little slut is my boy toy and life partner, Remy Boudreaux." He pronounced the French-sounding name *Boodrow*. "I picked him up in the Big Easy at the '72 Mardi Gras and haven't been able to get rid of him since." He grinned affectionately at the small man beside him and got an answering grin in return.

"And I guess you already know this tired old queen, since he's already been pesterin' you for your sexual history." Remy laid a small, shapely hand on Valenti's arm and gave him a dazzling smile. "You don't have to tell him if you don't want to, sugar. It's clear you haven't been in the scene long enough to be comfortable talkin' about it. Hell, if I met you on the street, I'da pegged you for straight as an arrow."

"Now, Remy, there you go messing things up. Charles here was all set to tell me all about himself, and you have to interfere." This time McGillis really did seem annoyed.

"Well, maybe he'd rather not talk about it. Look at him, sugar pie; he's just as pale as a ghost," Remy argued.

"No, that's okay. I don't mind, really," Valenti interrupted before they could really start arguing and draw attention to themselves, and him and his partner in the process. Did he really seem that straight? If so, their cover was in worse shape than he'd imagined, and he had to think fast. Maybe a suitably juicy "first time" story would shore up his image as a gay man. Then again, he had no idea what to say, and now both Paul and Remy were looking at him expectantly.

"Well, if you really don't mind telling, then I'd love to add your story to my book, Charles," McGillis said eagerly. "You don't have to go into details if you'd rather not. Just tell us about the man who initiated you into the joys of gay sex."

"I-I..." Valenti's mind was a total blank, and he felt like a fish out of water, with his mouth opening and closing and nothing coherent coming out.

"Actually, that was me." It was O'Brian's voice purring in his ear, and Valenti suddenly realized that his partner was practically sitting in his lap again and leaning around to speak to the men on his left.

"And you are?" Paul asked. He and Remy were both clearly intrigued by O'Brian's sudden appearance in the conversation.

"I'm Sean, Charles's partner," O'Brian said with a perfectly straight face, shaking hands with both of them.

"And you were the one who got him to come out?" Remy smiled shamelessly at his partner, and Valenti felt a sizzling jolt of jealousy as he realized the other man was interested in O'Brian, or at least found him attractive.

"Well," O'Brian said, still playing it cool. "We're actually not out at home yet. See, we're co-workers, have been for a long time."

"Is that right?" Paul seemed fascinated, and O'Brian nodded eagerly.

Valenti groaned inwardly. He knew all the signs of O'Brian in a story-telling mood. His partner was on a roll now, and who knew what elaborate yarn he'd spin. But strangely, he seemed to want to stick fairly close to the truth.

"Yeah, we've been co-workers for almost six years, been through a lot together in that time. We're from completely different backgrounds -- I'm just a Boston Irish kid from the wrong side of the tracks, and Valenti here grew up as Mister Moneybags in the Hamptons. But somehow the minute we met, we just clicked. It was like we completed each other -- like we were two halves of a whole, just waitin' to meet up." O'Brian ran one hand lovingly over Valenti's broad shoulder as he spoke.

"See, we're *more* than co-workers; we're best friends. Spend more time together than we do apart. We were always double dating -- blondes, brunettes, redheads -- the women all ran together after awhile. But at the end of the day, when the chips were down and everyone else was gone, I knew who I could depend on -- my partner, Valenti." Now his warm hand had wandered further over to the nape of Valenti's neck, and he squeezed and massaged rhythmically as he spoke.

"So how did this friendship turn into so much more, honey?" Remy's jewel-like eyes were even brighter as he asked the question that Valenti had been asking himself for the past month.

"Dunno, exactly." O'Brian paused and seemed to really consider this before continuing. "I guess I just woke up one day and realized I loved him -- *really* loved him, ya know? And our friendship was so close already, it just seemed to make sense to take it to the next level. I thought to myself, 'Why am I lookin' so hard to find all these special qualities in some woman when I've already found 'em in my best friend?' Valenti is the person I love most in the world. He gives me everything I need."

"Mmhm…" Paul and Remy both were nodding eagerly for him to continue, but Valenti wanted to shout, "Stop!" at the top of his lungs. It was too painful to have to sit there and listen to O'Brian tell the story that was no story for Valenti. He didn't want to be in this crazy place with his partner on his lap caressing him, touching him in ways he wanted to be touched so badly and could never hope to ask for under different circumstances. But he was stuck here, with no place to hide, and he had to listen and try to keep a straight face, no pun intended, as O'Brian went on.

"Well, one day I was givin' him a ride home from work in my car," his partner continued relentlessly, "and I decided enough was enough already. It was dark by the time we parked outside his place, so I figured no one was likely to see me make my move. He was about to get out of the car, and I said, 'Valenti.' He turned around to face me and said, 'What?' I said, 'This.' I pulled him in and well...I just kissed him." O'Brian's animated face was full of emotions that Valenti would have bet no one would be able to fake -- love, lust, wanting, need. *Oh, boy, Sean, you oughta get an Oscar for this one*, he thought miserably.

"Ooo, how did he react? Did he take a swing at you?" This was from Remy, who had obviously had some experience with kissing straight men.

"Nah." O'Brian grinned at Remy and Paul and cupped Valenti's cheek in one palm, absently caressing his partner's lips with one gentle thumb. "He *was* kinda shocked at first, though. His eyes got real wide, and he said, 'What the hell?' But then...then he grabbed me and kissed me back. Soft at first and then harder -- you get the idea." He grinned and nodded at the two men hanging on his words. Valenti had never known him to put so much thought and detail into a back-story before. It almost sounded like something that had really happened between them. He supposed that was the idea.

"Things got hot and heavy pretty quick, and I finally convinced him to come inside with me. I wanted to be together for the first time in his bed. Wanted to be surrounded by his scent, his touch." O'Brian went on relentlessly, and Valenti found that he was picturing everything his partner said in perfect detail. "We'd spent the night at each other's places a thousand times, you understand, but one or the other of us always slept on the couch. But that night we went straight to the bed.

"Things were a little strange at first. Neither Valenti or I had ever done anything like it before -- with another guy, I mean." O'Brian's eyes had a faraway look, and his pupils had dilated until the sea green was eaten almost entirely by drowning black. He looked like a man remembering the most erotic experience of his life. "He was on top, and then I was on top -- we didn't really have any idea exactly what to do. But I knew what I wanted right from the start, and I finally convinced him to let me try it."

Oh, God, is he really going to go into the gory details here? Valenti thought wildly. His partner shifted on his lap, and now that warm hand had slid down and slipped between two buttons to caress his chest under his shirt, coming dangerously close to a nipple. If O'Brian did much more of that, Valenti knew he wasn't going to be able to control his body's responses anymore.

"I unbuttoned his jeans and started pulling them down." O'Brian continued, much to his partner's discomfort. "And he was so big and hard, and it was such an enormous turn-on to know he'd gotten that way for me -- from me touching him and kissing him, ya know?" He shifted on Valenti's lap, and Valenti knew O'Brian *had* to be able to feel the huge erection he was now sporting pressed against his firm ass. But his partner just continued with the lurid details as though he hadn't noticed a thing.

"I took him in my hand and rubbed it -- the head -- all over my face. God, I'll never forget the sensation of holding him and touching him like that the first time. The skin was so soft, and he was rock-hard... I'm cut, but Valenti isn't, and I remember the way he looked so different from me, from anything I'd ever seen and yet so beautiful, too." O'Brian sighed and pressed even harder against Valenti's lap, pinning the imprisoned cock firmly between his round, tight cheeks as he spoke.

Valenti felt like his eyes were going to roll up in his head. He might explode if this went on much longer...but his partner was on a roll and seemingly unstoppable. And how did O'Brian know he was uncircumcised anyway? It wasn't like it was something they had ever discussed.

"I took a while to savor the feel of him in my hand and against my face. I loved the way he smelled -- spicy and hot. Then

I took him in my mouth and found out he tasted even better. By that time he was beggin' for it, clenchin' the bedspread in his fists all tense and tight... God, I almost came just from hearing the way he said my name as I took him down my throat..."

That was it -- Valenti felt he absolutely could not *stand* another word. He was going to have a coronary and die right here and now if O'Brian didn't stop talking and get off his lap.

"Uh, Sean? You're kind of squashing me here," he muttered through gritted teeth, pushing O'Brian firmly away.

"Huh? Oh, sorry, babe," O'Brian said absently, scooting over so that he was mostly in his own chair again. "Well, anyway," he said, leaning around Valenti to continue the conversation with Paul and Remy, "that's how it was. And we can't get enough of each other ever since."

"No, I should imagine not," Paul murmured, and Valenti thought that if he'd gotten any more turned on by O'Brian's bogus first-time story, the little round glasses perched on his nose would have steamed up.

"Well, that was gorgeous and *so* romantic." Remy grinned at them, also very affected by the story. "It'll be perfect for Paul's book." He sighed. "I just *love* a happy ending."

"Gets happier every night and no end in sight yet," O'Brian had the nerve to say before Valenti elbowed him sharply. "Ow, babe, what...?"

"Dessert," Valenti said shortly, and sure enough, the white-coated waiters were bringing around some kind of gooey chocolate confection that looked like it had about a thousand calories a bite. Valenti usually avoided anything this unhealthy, but he dug in with a relish he didn't feel in order to keep his mouth too full to talk, although he didn't taste a thing. Out of the corner of his eye, he saw his partner also digging in with apparent enjoyment.

It was with immense relief that he finally pushed back his plate and said cordial goodbyes to both Paul and Remy. At last the interminable meal was over. But his relief was short-lived, because as they pushed away from the table and prepared to go back to their room, he saw Conrad headed their way.

Chapter Seven

"I understand there was some trouble between your and two of my security team earlier today." Conrad, apparently not one for formalities, got to the point immediately, his cool shark's eyes flashing as he cornered them at the end of the massive dining hall.

"Yes, it was...most unfortunate," Valenti said coolly. "A misunderstanding on our part, but understandable, I think, since we're new to the RamJack."

"Understandable *if* you are who you say you are." Conrad frowned at both of them, sizing them up as he spoke. "Thaddeus, my chief of security, wasn't at all convinced of your...ah...orientation."

Valenti felt his partner tensing behind him, but he put a hand on O'Brian's shoulder, a gesture he had used a thousand times before. *Take it easy; I've got it covered.* O'Brian relaxed as he always did, his body language conveying his unshakable faith in his partner. Valenti hoped that faith wasn't misplaced this time.

"Are you saying we're here under false pretenses?" he demanded. *Might as well beard the lion in his den.*

"I am not saying anything -- yet," Conrad answered. "But you should be aware that the consequences for such actions could be...dire. Once or twice I have had some trouble of this kind -- reporters sneaking in, wanting an exclusive scoop on the gay life or the kink scene. I do not say you are in that league, but you should be aware that there are serious repercussions for such actions. Am I making myself clear?"

"Perfectly." Valenti felt his anger rising, or maybe it was just the frustrated lust he'd been fighting all night and for most of a month before that. "You think we're straight. Well, let me ask you, Mr. Conrad, how often do you see straight men doing this?" He turned suddenly to O'Brian, took his partner's face in his hands, and, with no warning, kissed him hard on the mouth.

At first he thought O'Brian wasn't going to respond and that their cover would be shot all to hell. *Come on, Sean*, he thought frantically. *Play along! You've got to play along...* And then his worries were pushed out of his head as his partner parted his lips and let Valenti's seeking tongue inside.

There was a shock of what could only be described as *rightness*, a feeling of belonging and possession so strong, he felt it down to his soul as he fed on those ripe red lips he'd been longing for so desperately, as he tasted O'Brian's hot mouth. Nearly groaning, Valenti bent to his task, pulling his partner more fully into his arms and pressing the lithe, firm body as close to his own as he could get it. He could feel O'Brian's arms winding around his waist as Valenti kissed him with all the pent-up passion that had been tormenting him all night.

There was nothing soft about it. It was a punishing kiss, a ravishing of his partner's mouth, meant to prove a point. What that point was, Valenti completely forgot the moment he gained entrance to O'Brian's sweet, chocolate-flavored mouth and the other man started kissing him back.

He heard a muffled groan from O'Brian, and then his partner was giving as good as he was getting, pressing against Valenti eagerly, slipping his own tongue inside Valenti's mouth to taste and explore in turn. Valenti became aware that his cock was rock hard and threatening to burst out of the conservative black suit pants, and his partner was in the same state as the kiss seemed to go on and on, rough and luscious and hot, until he though he would come on the spot just from tasting O'Brian's mouth.

They broke apart at last to come up for air, and Valenti finally remembered the reason he had been kissing his partner in the first place when he saw Conrad watching them dispassionately with those gray predator's eyes.

"That convince you?" Valenti asked, panting a little. His lips felt swollen and hot from the frenzied kiss, and his cock was throbbing desperately in his pants. He didn't dare look to see if O'Brian was in a similar state of discomfort.

"For now," Conrad replied. "But I will be keeping my eye on you, gentlemen. Try not to abuse my hospitality." Turning, he tossed over his shoulder, "Enjoy your stay at the RamJack. I will be seeing you later."

* * *

They were quiet until they got back to the room, and then, when the door was firmly shut and locked, Valenti turned to his partner and exploded.

"What the *hell* was that?" he demanded, advancing on the hapless O'Brian, who had the nerve to look surprised and uncomprehending.

"What was what?" O'Brian protested, putting up his hands in a "don't shoot" gesture to ward off his angry partner.

"That...that *story* you told back there!" Valenti nearly yelled, poking a finger into the solid chest before him.

"That, Nicky, was *me* keeping *you* from blowing our cover." O'Brian's eyes glinted dangerously as he began to get angry in turn. He grabbed Valenti's finger in one fist, pushing it away from his chest. "I had to say something quick to keep 'em from figuring out that we're not who we say we are."

"Well, did you have to go into such...*detail?*" Valenti demanded, still angry, but beginning to cool off a little now. His body was still throbbing from the effect of having O'Brian all over his lap and the passionate kiss they had just shared. He knew that his partner hadn't meant to torment him. O'Brian was just going undercover with the same single-minded devotion he brought to all their police work. It wasn't his fault that this particular assignment was driving Valenti over the edge.

"What was I gonna say?" O'Brian asked fiercely. His eyes were a hard green and narrowed in irritation. "I came up with the best thing I could; sorry it didn't meet your standards. Maybe next time I should leave you flappin' in the wind, but I can't do that, Valenti, because we're *partners.* We're s'posed to be watching out for each other, and that's all I was tryin' to do -- honest." He turned away and made as if to head into the bathroom to get some privacy, but Valenti caught his arm and pulled him back.

"No, wait, Sean. I-I'm sorry. I had no right to blow up at you that way. It's just that this whole situation is still freaking me out. And that story you told, well, it was so...realistic. So plausible..." His voice trailed off. How could he say that O'Brian had described exactly the kind of scenario he himself had been fantasizing about for the last month? He couldn't -- never in a million years could he admit that.

"It was *s'posed* to be plausible, Valenti. I thought that was the whole idea of tryin' to keep our names as close as possible and everything. The closer we stick to the truth, the less likely we are to slip up. You know that."

"I guess...it just sounded like something that could really happen." The minute the words were out of his mouth, he wanted to kick himself. Why had he put it that way?

"Sure it could happen, in the Bizarro universe." O'Brian whacked him on the shoulder in a friendly way obviously meant to ease the tension between them. "I'm sorry if it freaked you out,

Nick, but ya know, we're neck-deep in this thing now. It's kinda late to be gettin' homophobic on me."

"I know. I'm not," Valenti muttered, feeling like the biggest idiot in the world.

"Yeah, I guess not, what with that kiss you laid on me back there." O'Brian grinned and shook his head. "Man, I thought you were tryin' to perform a tonsillectomy on me right there in the dining room."

"I, uh, had to do something to prove to Conrad that we're trustworthy," Valenti protested.

"Yeah, I know you did. That whole little scene with him worries me -- seems like he might be on to us and we only just got here. I'm afraid we're gonna have to ramp up the act considerably tomorrow to be convincing, or he's never gonna agree to sell to us." O'Brian looked worried, and Valenti groaned inwardly to himself, wondering exactly what "ramping up the act" would entail. Would they have to kiss some more? Feel each other up? What? He had no clue and didn't want to ask, either.

"You mind if I get the first shower?" Valenti asked.

"Go head. I'm beat. Think I'm gonna just go straight to bed and hit the shower in the morning." O'Brian yawned hugely and began stripping off the tight black T-shirt and shorts in preparation for bed. Valenti hurriedly stepped into the bathroom and closed the door, trying not to think of his partner's muscular chest, the sight of which still lingered in his mind's eye.

When Valenti got out of the shower, O'Brian was already sprawled in the vast bed -- right in the middle, too, Valenti noted with some irritation. He guessed it was because his partner was used to sleeping alone. Valenti always took up the middle of the bed, as well, but tonight they were each going to have to pick a side and stick with it.

In the dim light from the room's one window, he noted the smooth line of his partner's body under the sheets and wondered if he was sleeping nude as usual. He knew that O'Brian did, had seen him naked often enough in the mornings after spending the night at his apartment, and had never thought anything about it before.

Valenti routinely slept in the raw, as well, although he wasn't sure he ought to tonight. Still, the thought of turning on the light and digging through the drawers in search of a pair of pajama bottoms wasn't very appealing. He was so tired -- emotionally and physically beat -- maybe he could just be sure to stay on his side of the bed...

"Nick?" O'Brian's voice, already fuzzy with sleep, floated to him through the darkness. "Come to bed, babe. 'S late." That warm, intimate tone decided Valenti, and he dropped the towel he'd been wearing around his waist to the floor and slid under the sheets beside his partner.

"Hey, O'Brian, shove over; you're taking your half out of the middle." Valenti nudged his partner, very aware of the warm, naked skin that brushed his as he did so.

"Yeah, yeah," O'Brian grumbled, moving over maybe two inches before settling again. Valenti tried to make himself comfortable in the limited space available to him, but he was still flank to flank with his partner, and he didn't want to roll over one way or the other for fear of brushing more sensitive areas together. *Be honest, Nicholas -- you want to be sure your cock doesn't brush his side.* Because despite an attempt to jerk off in the shower, Valenti was still rock hard, and being this close to his partner's naked body wasn't helping matters at all. He sighed and shifted minutely, trying to get more comfortable.

"Valenti?" His partner's voice in the darkness startled him so much that he nearly fell out of bed. He had thought O'Brian was asleep.

"Yeah?" he asked, feeling his heart pound in his chest from the sudden fright. "What's up, partner?"

"Well." O'Brian rolled over onto his side, and Valenti turned his head and found himself looking into two pools of darkness that he knew were O'Brian's eyes. "I been thinkin'."

"Shouldn't do that, O'Brian -- you might blow a fuse or something." Valenti tried to sound natural.

"Ha-ha, Nicky, you're a regular laugh riot. Look, I'm tryin' to be serious here, okay?"

"Okay," Valenti whispered. "I'm sorry. You're worried about the case, right? About our cover?"

"Yeah..." His partner sighed and made a movement that Valenti knew meant he was running a hand through his hair. "Ya know -- you were worried about blowing our cover tonight, but you actually did pretty good. I mean, that kiss was a stroke of genius."

"You think?" Valenti asked uncertainly. "I wasn't sure if Conrad bought it or not. It's not like I really knew what I as doing..."

"I know, and that's the problem. God knows what we'll have to do tomorrow or the next day to pull this thing off, and we don't know the first thing about how to go about it. With each other, I mean." O'Brian's voice was low and worried in the darkness, and Valenti had to admit he was probably right.

"Yeah... But what can we do? It's not like we get a lot of practice kissing other guys," Valenti pointed out, rolling over to face his partner in the dark.

"That's exactly the problem, Nick -- we don't know 'cause we don't get any practice. Now, don't get me wrong, it's not something I *wanna* be practicing as a general thing, but this time -- well, I think we might have to make an exception."

"Sean, what *exactly* are you talking about?" Valenti felt as though two billion butterflies had suddenly taken up residence in his stomach, and he was getting that can't-get-a-deep-enough-breath feeling again as he considered his partner's words. What exactly did O'Brian want to do? And how far did he want to go with it?

"I'm talkin' about kissing, Valenti. Just kissing." O'Brian replied a little too hastily, and Valenti noticed that he had backpedaled to the use of Valenti's last name, as well. "You did a terrific job tonight, but you caught me off-guard, and I bet my reactions showed it," O'Brian continued. "I though maybe we should practice a little -- just to make it look more natural tomorrow, ya know?"

"Well, I guess..." Valenti tried to sound reluctant, as though kissing his partner was the last thing he wanted to do. "Um...how do we start?"

"By getting a little closer, for one thing." O'Brian's tone was so matter-of-fact that it dispelled a lot of Valenti's nervousness, and he closed the gap between them less awkwardly than he could have imagined possible. O'Brian looped an arm around his neck, and the two men lay close in the darkness, their upper bodies touching, although there was still plenty of room between them from the waist down.

"Now what?" Valenti asked nervously. Feeling the warmth of his partner's skin, the wiry mat of hair on O'Brian's chest rubbing against his own smooth chest, was startlingly erotic, and he could feel his body beginning to react helplessly to the stimulation.

"Now I'm gonna kiss you, babe," O'Brian breathed in his ear, and that was all the warning Valenti got before those hot, full lips covered his and he was tasting his partner's mouth for the second time that night.

Their first kiss in front of Conrad had been hungry and forceful, Valenti pouring out his frustration and need as he took his partner's mouth ruthlessly. But now, with O'Brian doing the kissing, he found it was softer -- still strong and demanding, but gentle at the same time. Almost as though his partner was asking him to open himself to the kiss, to give himself up to the experience and let go of his doubt and shame for a while and just enjoy what was happening.

Valenti responded wholeheartedly -- how could he not? He was naked in bed with his best friend -- the man he loved most in the whole world, and he had been given carte blanche to show his feelings without having to worry about the consequences and repercussions of his actions.

He found that he was kissing O'Brian back -- *more* than kissing him back. He was exploring his partner's mouth, tasting him, taking him, *owning* him in a way that he had never been able to do before. His hands roved over scratchy, warm skin, connecting with a sleek, naked flank...a flat, furry chest...well-muscled arms. O'Brian's body was firm and muscular -- satisfying to touch and caress and completely unlike the smooth, hairless skin and soft, yielding form of a woman.

"Whoa, babe..." O'Brian's breathless voice broke his trance, and Valenti became suddenly aware that he had rolled the smaller man under him and was pinning his partner firmly to the mattress. He was holding O'Brian's arms over his head, and the compact, muscular body was stretched out under Valenti's own lankier frame. Valenti's cock, as hard as a bar of lead, was rubbing against his partner's shaft, which was in a similar state of arousal.

"Oh, God," he mumbled, mortified.

Releasing his partner's wrists, he tried to roll away, but O'Brian held him firmly in place, wrapping his arms around Valenti's back, and whispered, "Wait a minute, Nicky. Where do you think you're goin'?"

"Anywhere else but here. God, Sean -- don't know what came over me. Guess it's been too long between girls. I'm sorry." Valenti tried to roll away again, but his partner refused to allow it. Still holding his partner tight in his arms, O'Brian opened his legs to cradle Valenti between his thighs. Valenti felt a long sigh fall out of himself as O'Brian gently rocked against him, rubbing their hard cocks together in an excruciatingly hot rhythm.

"What...what are you doing?" Valenti gasped, unable to stop himself from responding to his partner's stroking. Both cocks were leaking freely now, and the warm layer of pre-cum was helping to generate delicious friction between them. Much more of this, and he would explode -- would come all over his partner's flat belly, and he knew he couldn't do that.

"I'm just practicin'," O'Brian whispered in his ear, using one hand on the back of his neck to draw Valenti down into another long, breathless kiss and explore his partner thoroughly. "Feels nice, doesn't it?"

"Yeah, but..." Valenti struggled to remember why they shouldn't be doing this, but his partner's body against his felt too wonderful to deny. Groaning, he pumped back, feeling the length of his shaft rub against O'Brian's from its thick base to the wide, flaring head. It felt like velvet over hot steel.

"We might have to do this or worse." O'Brian's voice in his ear sounded breathless and low. "Better get the awkwardness out of the way now. Right?" His hips continued to work as he talked, driving Valenti to distraction -- nearly over the edge and beyond.

"Right, I guess..." Valenti gasped and leaned down to capture O'Brian's mouth with his once more, loving the taste of the man beneath him and the feel of his best friend's solid, aching cock against his own. "But, Sean...we keep this up, I'm gonna come. Can't...can't help it..."

He felt closer to the edge with each passing second, and it was the most sublime feeling he could ever imagine. No quick roll in the hay with any woman had ever been half as good as this intense pleasure he was sharing with his partner, the man of his heart, who was rocking beneath him -- offering his body for their mutual bliss.

"That's okay. Hell, more than okay. I'm close, too," O'Brian whispered back. "C'mon, babe, wanna feel you come. Wanna come with you..." He gave a particularly strong thrust against Valenti's cock, and the combination of those hot words and the achingly wonderful friction pushed Valenti over the edge. Groaning, he wrapped his arms around his partner and held O'Brian tight as fierce spasms shook him and hot cum spurted between their bodies. He felt the man beneath him tremble, and then O'Brian was coming, too, arching against him helplessly and gasping his name. *Nick, oh, God, Nick*, over and over as he let himself go.

For a long moment they lay together, not speaking, too tired and emotionally wiped to even attempt coherent conversation. Slowly, though, the realization of what he had done began to come back to Valenti. He had come all over his best friend's belly, had rubbed against him like a cat in heat until he spurted hot cum all over O'Brian. True, O'Brian had done the same thing, had even encouraged him to let go and let it happen, but maybe that had just been the heat of passion talking. Would he hate Valenti now that it was done and over with? Would he want nothing more to do with him? Valenti lay there, frozen on top of his partner, waiting for O'Brian's Irish-Catholic values to reassert themselves with a vengeance.

"Oof, you're heavy." O'Brian's good-natured complaint dispelled some of Valenti's fears as he rolled hurriedly off his partner. He knew O'Brian inside and out, and if the other man was upset about what had just happened between them, he would have let Valenti know at once.

"Sorry," Valenti mumbled. "Made a mess..." He began to get up to go to the bathroom and get cleaned up, but O'Brian's hand on his arm held him in place.

"Hey, it's half mine, ya know, babe. Stay where you are. I'll rinse up and get you a washcloth." His partner hopped nimbly off the bed and went into the bathroom before Valenti could protest.

He lay in the half-light and listened to the sounds of water splashing in the basin and some other sound he couldn't quite identify. Finally the water sounds stopped, and he realized with growing incredulity that O'Brian was actually *humming*. Apparently the thing they had just done together -- Valenti couldn't quite bring himself to call it sex -- didn't bother his partner at all.

Valenti didn't know whether to be relieved or irritated about that. Then again, O'Brian could afford to be relaxed; to him this was just a practice run -- *Can't exactly call it a dry run -- ha-ha, Nicholas, very funny* -- for what they might have to do while they were here at the RamJack. He wasn't nearly as emotionally invested in this new physical aspect of their relationship as Valenti was.

Lying in the dark and listening to his partner hum off-key in the bathroom, Valenti felt a deep yearning within himself, a longing to tell O'Brian everything. How he felt, what he had been thinking, but most of all how much he loved and needed the man. Like two halves of a whole, his partner had said, and that summed it up perfectly for Valenti. But it could never be. This was nothing to his partner -- just another part of the job.

Valenti felt like a black hole had opened in his chest at the realization -- a bleak void that sucked all his hope and happiness away with a terrible finality. He could never reveal himself or declare his love to his partner; what was the use? He put an arm over his eyes and fought back the blue headache that wanted to turn into tears.

"Hey, Nicky, you okay?" O'Brian's voice in his ear startled him, and Valenti dropped the arm to his side and tried to look normal.

"Yeah, sure. Just...tired. You got that washcloth?" he asked, becoming aware that his thighs and belly were still covered in a thin layer of sticky cum. He reached out a hand toward his partner; the bathroom light was still on, and he could clearly see that O'Brian held something in his fist.

"Nah, babe. Let me," O'Brian whispered, his voice low and gentle. Before Valenti could answer, O'Brian was kneeling down by his thighs, and a warm, wet sensation was traveling along the length of Valenti's body as O'Brian stroked him softly with the washcloth. Valenti felt tense, at first, but the feeling of the warm cloth and O'Brian's hands -- so infinitely gentle and tender on his body -- were soothing, and at last he simply relaxed and let himself float hazily as he watched his partner work.

O'Brian was nothing if not thorough, and after Valenti's thighs and belly were clean, O'Brian took his partner's still semi-erect shaft in one hand and stroked the washcloth along its sensitive length as Valenti watched in wonder. Could this really be his partner doing this? Handling him so easily, as though he'd done it all his life, as thought they were partners in every sense of the word?

"Sean, I..." he began, but his partner shushed him with one finger pressed gently against Valenti's lips. Then he bent his head low, and Valenti gasped at the feel of the wet warmth enveloping the flaring head of his cock. Despite his recent orgasm, he felt his shaft try to spring to life at that intimate kiss, twitching helplessly as O'Brian tongued and sucked him gently, holding him in that hot mouth for an endless moment before releasing him reluctantly and giving the wide, plum-shaped head one last open-mouthed kiss.

For a moment Valenti was speechless, and then he managed to say, "What...?" His hands itched to pull his partner's head back down and feed his hard shaft between those warm, willing lips again, but he sensed the moment had passed.

"Missed some." O'Brian shrugged, as though he sucked Valenti's cock every day of the week and it was no big deal. Suddenly, his partner's words of just that afternoon came back to Valenti. "I'll be your boy, but don't expect me to suck your dick," O'Brian had said, just kidding around. But here they were not twenty-four hours later, and he was doing exactly that. Valenti shivered convulsively.

"Sean…" he started to say, but his partner was already cuddled under the covers, turning his back to Valenti and obviously trying to get to sleep.

"Try not to worry about it, Nick," he advised sleepily as he nudged back against Valenti's body so that his ass was cradled against his partner's crotch. "It's just things we have to get used to in order to solve this case. Gotta do whatever it takes. Just try not to stress over it, 'kay?"

"Okay, I guess…" Valenti mumbled. Despite the turmoil in his mind, the orgasm he had experienced had drained him utterly, and he could feel sleep sucking him under no matter how he tried to escape it. Well, maybe O'Brian was right…and maybe he should be grateful for this opportunity to touch and be touched by his partner in such forbidden ways while it lasted. The minute Conrad sold to them and they busted him, the assignment would be over, and he would have to content himself once more with the purely platonic friendship he was used to with O'Brian.

Valenti wound his arms around the smaller man in front of him and pulled O'Brian close. Shutting his eyes, he gave in to sleep.

Chapter Eight

He woke up to feel his morning hard-on nestled securely between the firm cheeks of his partner's ass. *Hmmm, nice...* He kissed the vulnerable nape of O'Brian's neck just under the bright thatch of reddish-blond hair and rocked gently against him, loving the feeling of the lush ass pressing against his shaft. O'Brian, reacting to the stimulation, pressed back against him, rubbing along his length with a low moan.

Still half asleep, Valenti did what came naturally. He pressed against O'Brian's body and reached around his partner's hips to capture O'Brian's hard cock in one hand.

"Mmmm..." O'Brian was practically purring as he thrust into the warm circle of his partner's hand, responding to the firm grip Valenti had on his shaft. The soft noise penetrated the sleep-induced fog in Valenti's brain, and things began to register. In a blinding moment of clarity, he realized this was *not* a dream; he actually *was* pumping his cock against his partner's ass and stroking O'Brian off at the same time. The tight ass against his shaft and the hard cock in his hand both felt incredibly right, but Valenti suddenly realized that the whole situation was utterly wrong.

"Oh, God!" He let O'Brian go and pushed violently away from his partner, actually falling off the bed in his attempt to distance himself.

"Wha...?" O'Brian's sleepy green eyes appeared over the edge of the bed, and he peered groggily at Valenti lying on his back on the floor. "What you doin' down there, Valenti?" he asked, blinking owlishly. "Was havin' this incredible dream, and then all of a sudden I woke up and you weren't there."

"I don't know...I just...I fell off." Valenti couldn't bring himself to tell his partner that the dream had been no dream. "Time for breakfast anyway," he said, glancing up at the bedside clock. "Actually, it's nearly time for lunch. Must've forgotten to set the alarm. We overslept."

"Oh, shit!" O'Brian was instantly awake and leaping out of bed to grab a quick shower. "What's wrong with us, Valenti? We never oversleep when we're on an assignment," he grumbled through the bathroom door.

Yes, but we never kiss each other and come all over each other, either. Or suck each other... As he dressed hurriedly, grateful he had taken a shower the night before, Valenti shivered at the vividly sensual memory of O'Brian's mouth surrounding the head of his cock. *What are we coming to? Pun not intended -- very funny, Nicholas. Undercover or not, this kind of thing will change our relationship forever -- there's just no way it can't.* When he finished dressing, he sat on the bed and waited for his partner to emerge from the shower.

In five minutes O'Brian came out, his thick reddish-gold hair still dripping, with only a towel wrapped around his lean hips. He rummaged through the drawers, humming to himself as he looked for a fresh twinkie outfit to put on. As O'Brian pulled on the tight shorts and tank top, Valenti tried in vain not to watch his partner's ass and think what he wanted to say. They had to talk about this -- about what was happening between them. He loved O'Brian, loved touching him, but more than anything he didn't want to damage their partnership.

Finally, O'Brian turned around, toweling his hair vigorously and revealing a bright red shirt that looked great with his golden skin tones. In black block letters, the shirt proclaimed, "You say Tomato, I say Fuck Off." It took a moment to register, and when it did Valenti tried to keep a straight face, tried to keep his mind on what he needed to talk about with his partner, but the damn shirt was just too much. Before he knew it, the brittle tension inside him had broken into a million pieces, and he was holding his sides and howling with laughter.

"What? Is it my hair?" O'Brian played dumb, clearly amused by his partner's reaction to the slogan on his tank. Finally Valenti's laughter tapered off to snickers and the occasional chuckle, and he shook his head and pointed at the shirt.

"Where?" he asked simply.

"From the Louvre on my last trip to gay Paree," O'Brian answered, grinning. "'S the only place they sell 'em. Limited edition, ya know."

"God, Sean -- you're too much." Valenti wiped tears out of his eyes, feeling better, although nothing had been said. Maybe, he reflected, it was better to just let things lie -- at least for now.

"Didn't you say it was time for lunch?" his partner demanded, looking at the clock. "I'm hungry, Valenti. Let's get goin'."

"After you." Valenti gestured toward the solid oak door, still grinning a little, and his partner sashayed past him, clearly already in character and ready to tackle another day. But just as Valenti was about to open the door and usher him into the hall, O'Brian turned with a serious expression on his fine-featured face. The sea-green eyes reminded Valenti of the ocean after a storm.

"Listen, partner, don't forget out there -- we're a team. Whatever we have to do, it's all part of the game plan to bring Conrad down -- got it?"

"Hey, Sean, spare me the pep talk. I know what we're doing and why," Valenti protested lamely. But his partner's eyes wouldn't let him go.

"You sure about that? Because we can't let anything they throw at us divide us, Nick. Us against them, partner. Right?" He put one hand on Valenti's cheek, tilting the taller man's facedown to make his point.

"Always, partner. Us against the world, and I'm betting on us," Valenti replied sincerely, loving the warm touch of his partner's hand on his face. Loving O'Brian with his whole heart. He hoped the emotion didn't show too much on his face.

"Good." O'Brian peered at him intently and then did something that surprised Valenti, although not as much as it might have a day ago. He leaned up and kissed Valenti very softly on the mouth, taking his time to let his partner know how he felt with the sweet pressure of his lips.

It was as though O'Brian had flipped a light switch somewhere inside his body. Valenti felt his cock grow rigid and heard himself groan low in his throat. Then he was opening his lips and welcoming his partner's tongue inside, relearning the taste of Sean O'Brian all over again. At last the blond man pulled back, and he still looked as serious as he had before the kiss.

"Love you, babe," he said shortly. "Don't forget it out there."

"Back at you, partner," Valenti said in a low voice, caressing the smooth cheek briefly before letting his hand drop back to the doorknob. O'Brian gave one final nod, and then they headed out to do their jobs.

* * *

Lunch was a quiet, informal affair, and Valenti knew without being told that today was their day to case the joint, to mingle and reinforce their image as a gay couple. Not until tomorrow would they attempt to buy any coke unless the perfect opportunity came their way. But after catching a glowering glance from the blond security goon, whom he supposed had to be Thad, Valenti didn't think that was likely. They finished their food and got up from the table, pausing briefly to wave at Paul and Remy before strolling out of the dining hall together.

"What now?" Valenti muttered, staying close to his partner as they walked down the opulent expanse of hallway. Parquet wood floors were polished to a high gloss, and every room they passed was decorated with impeccable taste.

"I think we should check out the Basement." O'Brian jerked his head in the direction of a long flight of stairs descending into gloom at the end of the hall. "That's where all the action in this place is going down -- I'd bet my badge on it."

"Yeah?" *What kind of action?* But Valenti didn't say it out loud. As O'Brian had said, they would do what they had to do, regardless. He eyed the ominous stairs with a sardonic eye. He supposed the dimmer lighting and darker colors were meant to make the stairs leading to the Basement seem dangerous -- risky territory. Ambiance was everything in a place like this, and the RamJack certainly didn't disappoint.

"C'mon." O'Brian started down the stairs, trailing one hand along the cool, gray marble banister, heading for the small black door at the bottom. The door was simple and unadorned except for letters stenciled in white on its black surface: THE VIEWING ROOM, THE DARK KNIGHT, and THE MINOTAUR'S LAIR, Valenti read as O'Brian reached for the silver knob. He was beginning to get a really bad feeling about this part of the RamJack. At least two of the names on the door sounded familiar, and all three sounded ominous. *Didn't Twonnie warn us about some of these areas?*

"Hey, Sean, you sure about this?" he said, casting his partner a worried look.

"Sure. Long as we stick together, we can't go wrong." O'Brian nodded with a self-assurance Valenti wished he felt and pulled open the door. Behind it was a short stretch of dark hallway leading to a round room with a high, vaulted ceiling. The walls and floor were made of gray stone that sweated moisture and echoed the least noise back to them. The impression of being in an underground labyrinth was completed by the dim lighting from medieval-looking wall sconces and the three arching doorways leading off in separate directions from the round central room.

Standing guard at the center of the round room was the black-haired goon with the gravelly voice from yesterday. From the look on his side-of-beef face, his disposition hadn't improved any in the interval since they had seen him last.

"Back again, twink?" he asked O'Brian with a nasty grin. "Just can't get enough, can you?"

"Just bein' near you is enough for me, handsome," O'Brian replied sarcastically.

"You mind your P's and Q's, boy, or I'll get a lot nearer than you want." The goon towered over Valenti's partner, doing his best to look menacing, but O'Brian just shrugged it off.

Valenti knew his partner was used to being underestimated by taller, beefier guys all the time because of his compact frame. Those same guys were always surprised when they ended up with their faces in the dirt and O'Brian's cuffs around their wrists. Unfortunately, they couldn't resort to that kind of action here. He realized that he should be playing the part of the protective sponsor, not just standing by and letting his partner shoot off his mouth like he usually did.

Stepping closer to O'Brian, he wrapped an arm around his partner's shoulders and caressed his chest with one hand. Leaning down, he planted a kiss on the corner of O'Brian's full mouth and gave the goon a glare that plainly said, *Back off -- he's mine.*

"Where do you want to go, Sean?" he asked, nuzzling his cheek against the soft reddish-blond hair.

"Mmm, I think we should check out the Viewing Room," O'Brian answered, turning his head to return the kiss with interest.

"You can't go there. Viewing Room's closed since there's no show going on." The goon looked bored, as though he'd been saying the same thing to different men all morning. Valenti wondered if he was hiding anything. Naturally the place they weren't supposed to go was where they probably needed to be. But maybe they should save a foray to the Viewing Room for later.

"When's the next show, then?" O'Brian asked, never willing to let things drop.

"Don't know." The goon gave them a shark-like grin and adjusted his tight leather pants purposefully. "Whenever Conrad says. You want to watch yourself while you're here, or you could be the next show yourself, twink."

"Always wanted to be a star." O'Brian blew the goon a kiss and nodded at the far left archway that was labeled THE DARK KNIGHT. "Let's try in there. I checked out the Minotaur's Lair yesterday before tall, dark, and ugly kicked me out."

"I was saving that tight ass of yours, twinkie." The goon leered at the anatomy in question, and Valenti found that he didn't have to fake the possessive glare he shot the man's way this time. "The Minotaur's no place for a sweet little virgin like you."

"I can take care of myself, buddy. I was doin' just fine without you," O'Brian said shortly, and Valenti sensed his partner's patience with the goon's snide remarks was running out. He pulled O'Brian closer to him, hoping to avoid a full-on confrontation. To his surprise, though, his partner's words finally seemed to have some effect on the man in front of them.

"Yeah, I saw the way you handled those guys. Not bad for a twink," he said grudgingly. "But you want to remember something, sweetheart. I don't know what you are on the outside, but here at the RamJack, with your sweet little ass on display, you ain't nothin' but fresh meat. Got it?"

"We get the picture," Valenti replied quickly, heading for the archway marked THE DARK KNIGHT and practically dragging O'Brian with him. "I won't leave Sean alone again."

"Make sure you don't," the goon growled after them. "Your boy made several enemies down here yesterday, and I don't wanna have to clean up any messes."

As they went under the archway and down another short, dark hall, Valenti spun around to face O'Brian and hissed, "I can't believe you came down here alone yesterday. What exactly happened, anyway?"

O'Brian shrugged. "Nothin' much. Some of the guys in that Minotaur room were interested in me. But since I'm savin' my sweet ass for you, *I* wasn't interested in *them*. We had a disagreement, which tall, dark, and ugly back there broke up. He's just mad that I snuck in right under his nose."

"Still, this isn't the kind of place you should go without back-up, partner," Valenti reminded him gently, deciding not to comment on the "sweet ass" remark. "From now on we stick together so I can get your back."

"Funny," O'Brian said dryly, "That's exactly the part of me those guys in the Minotaur wanted to get. Or maybe a little lower, if ya know what I mean." He winked at his partner and grinned sarcastically.

Valenti slapped his ass. "Do not get fresh, boy," he warned in a cold voice -- a dead-on imitation of Conrad from the night before. "Your attitude leaves much to be desired."

"Ooo, forgive me, Master," O'Brian cracked, grinning at him and running one hand over the tight jean shorts provocatively. "Are you gonna punish me? Should I be waiting on the bed on my hands and knees for you to fuck me?"

The words sent a jolt of lust straight to Valenti's groin, and suddenly the situation wasn't funny anymore.

"Don't, Sean..." He wet his lips; suddenly, his mouth seemed too dry to talk. "Don't joke about that. Not here, okay?"

"What's the matter, Nicky? You look like you seen a ghost. I'm just kiddin', ya big lug. Put it outta your head -- never gonna happen. Now, c'mon, we got work to do." O'Brian clapped his partner on the shoulder and led the way to the end of the hall and through a black door with the words THE DARK KNIGHT scripted in dripping red.

Chapter Nine

"Well, they didn't spare any expense with the decorations in here," Valenti said sarcastically. Actually, the Dark Knight appeared to be a kind of a bar, and it was more simply furnished than any room he had seen yet at the opulent resort.

Dim lighting picked up the black walls and ceiling, making the room sweatingly claustrophobic. A long, polished counter of black marble ran the length of the room, and behind it a brooding bald man with biceps the size of Valenti's head was morosely wiping at shot glasses with a tiny white towel. A few tables were scattered around, and several men sat at them, sipping various drinks and talking in low voices.

"This is it?" Valenti whispered to his partner, pretending to lean down and kiss him on the neck as he spoke. "This is the scary place Twonnie warned us about? There's nothing going on here."

"Uh, babe, I think all the action's in there." O'Brian pointed to a corner of the room Valenti hadn't noticed before. He saw a doorway covered by a long, black leather curtain. Now that he listened, he could hear what sounded like music and other noises coming from behind that ominous length of leather. "You comin'?" O'Brian was already moving toward the doorway, and Valenti sighed in resignation.

"Right behind you," he said, squaring his shoulders. Together they pushed back the surprisingly heavy curtain and entered another world.

The first thing Valenti saw when he entered the dim back room was a wide movie screen that seemed to cover most of the back wall. On it, somewhat predictably, a gay porno was playing. *Guess* Heidi *wasn't available*, Valenti thought, grinning a little. The two men on the screen certainly seemed to be enjoying their jobs. The dark-haired actor was sucking and licking his blond partner's dick enthusiastically, and as they watched, he engulfed the entire shaft in his mouth down to the balls as the other man moaned and grasped at his hair.

"Wow, they're really goin' for it." O'Brian sounded awed -- maybe even a little impressed at this act of sexual bravado. "Wonder how he does that?"

"More to the point, what's the Viewing Room for if they show movies like this in here?" Valenti whispered back.

"Dunno, maybe it's for..."

O'Brian didn't get to finish his thought because suddenly a huge meat hook of a hand engulfed the back of his neck and a low, growling voice behind them said, "Well, if it isn't the little tease from yesterday. I got a present for you, blondie, and I promised myself I was gonna give it to you if I saw you again."

Valenti looked up the arm connected to the beefy hand on his partner's neck to see its owner. Standing over them was the most enormous man he had ever seen; he made the bartender outside look like a lightweight. A low hairline and a jutting shelf of a jaw made the man look more than a little like a Neanderthal, and small, piggy eyes of indeterminate color reinforced the image.

Turning his head further, Valenti could see that this fine specimen of primitive man was wearing no shirt. Tattooed across his heavily muscled chest were the words "Jesus is coming- Look busy." *Boy, Sean, you sure know how to pick 'em*, he thought with resignation. They stood no chance against this guy in a fight; it would be like throwing a punch at a brick wall. But Valenti had to try.

"Back off -- he's mine," he said as confidently as he could. The bullet head swiveled on its thick neck, and Valenti could've sworn he heard tendons creaking as the man moved.

"He's yours, huh? Well, I'm sure you don't mind sharin', now, do you?"

"I said, he's *mine*." Valenti's hand itched for his Python. The snub nose of Valenti's pistol jammed in his ribs might have given Mr. Cro-Magnum second thoughts about this kind of action. But, of course, they couldn't go armed inside the resort, and his fist clenched on empty air -- they were on their own here. The enormous man let go of O'Brian, who was glaring at him, and moved toward Valenti, who braced himself.

"Come on, Harry -- you know the rules." A tiny man with a puckish face and a shock of bright, carroty hair was suddenly between them, a hand on either chest, although he really had to reach to get higher than the Neanderthal's belt buckle. He was also dressed from head to toe in leather, as was nearly every man in the room, Valenti realized. *Mutt and Jeff,* he thought dazedly, looking from the midget to the giant and back again. "If the twink has a sponsor, you can't touch him."

"I'm gonna do more than touch 'im, Peter," growled the huge man. "I'm gonna fuck his sweet ass till he screams for more." He grinned, more a baring of teeth than an expression of genuine amusement. "Reckon it might take me a while."

Where are we, a bad prison movie? Valenti wondered dismally. He could feel himself sweating, could feel O'Brian's anger like a line of heat along his spine, but he couldn't let his partner take an active hand in this -- it would be completely out of character. He just hoped O'Brian realized it. Valenti was supposed to the protector here -- the Master, the sponsor. The realization bolstered his courage.

"You touch him, I'll kill you," he snarled, surprised to find that he really meant it. "I mean it. I will rip your fucking head off, man. I'm not telling you again. *He's mine.*"

He stepped forward, feeling a rage he hadn't known was in him at the thought of someone threatening to do *that* to his partner. *If anybody's gonna fuck you, Sean, it's gonna be me.* The thought appalled him, but the proprietary emotions refused to fade. O'Brian was *his*, goddammit. And he'd be damned if anyone else laid so much as a finger on his partner.

Growling something incoherent, the immense man stepped forward and grasped a handful of the button-down shirt Valenti was wearing. *Not dressed right for the scene*, Valenti thought absently. *Gotta buy a pair of leather pants to fit in with this crowd.*

"Whoa, boys. Take it easy now. Harry, you know how Mr. Conrad dislikes unauthorized violence on his premises." It was the tiny red-haired man again, pushing between them fearlessly, although Valenti could have crushed him with one hand, let alone what the Neanderthal he was facing could have done. He half expected the huge man to turn and swat the little guy like a fly, but to his surprise, the ham-sized fist slowly relaxed its grip on his shirt, and "Harry" stepped back.

"Fine, I won't fuck 'im." He sounded positively sullen, Valenti thought, like a little boy pouting for a toy he couldn't have. "But if they won't give us a taste, they should at least have to put on a show. Make 'em enter one of the contests, Peter." There were murmurs of agreement from the crowd of thirty or so men who had gathered around to see the action.

"Oh, yes, a hot-looking pair like that -- better than a porno." This from a middle-aged man who was also wearing a pair of leather pants. He turned to the man behind him, who was obviously his "boy," and Valenti saw that strategically placed holes had been cut in the pants. Pale, doughy cheeks flashed him, and he looked away quickly, trying to hide a smile. The adrenaline in his system was beginning to fade a little, leaving him feeling shaky and relieved. Apparently he wasn't going to have to do the Texas two-step with the Neanderthal after all.

"Peek-a-boo," O'Brian muttered; the pants had also caught his attention. "Gotta get you some pants like that, babe," his partner continued in a low voice meant for Valenti's ears alone. "You'd fill 'em out better, I'm sure."

"Shut up. You're not helping any," Valenti said from the corner of his mouth. Clearing his throat, he turned to the tiny man named Peter. "What contests? We're new here," he explained. "Although my, uh, boy wandered down here yesterday by mistake."

"Yes, I can see that. You two might as well have 'fresh meat' written all over you in big red letters." The little man took in Valenti's button-down shirt and pressed pants with an expression of disapproval.

"Look." He took Valenti by the elbow and led him to a quiet corner, O'Brian trailing behind them. "Don't you know that the Dark Knight is the leather part of the RamJack? Just by coming down here, you're acknowledging that you want to play rough. The guys down here don't always take no for an answer."

"I kind of got that impression from your large friend over there," Valenti said dryly, nodding at the Neanderthal.

"Oh, Harry? He's harmless." The little man made a dismissive gesture with his hand. "But there are a few more down here that you want to watch out for. You can really get hurt if you don't know what you're doing.

"What's this contest he was talkin' about?" O'Brian came up beside Valenti and wrapped a proprietary arm around his waist, leaning into him so that Valenti could feel O'Brian's body heat all along his right side.

"That's just a little fun we like to have. You're not really dressed for it, of course, but you're welcome to participate. The contests down here are open to all *comers*." He grinned at them and nodded his head toward a small stage set against the far wall. "The blowjob contest is going to start in a few minutes, and after that there's the Wankathon."

"Wankathon?" Valenti shook his head -- had he heard the man correctly?

"A jerk-off contest," Peter explained. "We have prizes for the fastest time, the slowest time, and the best technique." He shrugged as though it was all standard procedure.

"Um, I think we're going to take a pass this time," Valenti said, turning to his partner. "Right, Sean?"

"I think we should do it," O'Brian said unexpectedly.

"What?" Valenti felt as though his partner had punched him in the stomach. "You think we should *what?*"

"Look." O'Brian took him by the arm with a nod of apology to Peter and pulled him close to whisper in his ear. "Don't you see, Nicky? This is the golden opportunity we've been looking for to secure our cover once and for all. If we really put on a show, the whole damn place'll hear about it, and there's no way Conrad will suspect us of being straight."

"I'm beginning to wonder about us myself," Valenti muttered, which earned him a blank look from his partner. "But, O'Brian, there's no way I'm going to blow you or...or let you blow me in front of this crowd of perverts. There are *limits*." He could feel the hot blush creeping over his face as he talked; he couldn't help remembering the brief touch of his partner's mouth on his cock the night before. If O'Brian was thinking along similar lines, his face didn't show it.

"Who said anything about blowjobs, Valenti?" he argued. "Peter there said there was a jerk-off contest, too."

"The Wankathon? You want to enter the Wankathon?" The unreality of what he was saying washed over Valenti, and he had an almost insurmountable urge to burst into laughter. The corners of his mouth twitched despite his best efforts, and suddenly he was snickering like a kid. O'Brian took one look at his partner and started laughing, too.

"Yeah," he managed to say between snorts of laughter. "I wanna join the Wankathon. I'm gonna be king of the Wankathon, babe. Bet I set a new wanking record."

"Sean, be serious," Valenti pleaded, trying to get a grip on himself. He was glad they were hidden away in the corner, where not many people could see them cutting up like a couple of school kids.

"I *am* being serious," O'Brian insisted. "Look, babe, I know it's not your thing, so I'm not askin' you to do it. But I can get up there and choke the chicken with the best of 'em if it means we take Conrad down in flames. You have to admit it would really help our cover."

"Yeah, it would, but are you *sure*?" Valenti frowned, not liking the idea of dozens of pairs of hungry eyes on a part of O'Brian he had yet to really look at himself. His partner shrugged.

"Sure, I'm sure. I'd do worse than that to get this bastard. You grab us a seat. I'm gonna go tell Peter I'll do it."

O'Brian headed back toward the little man who seemed to be the unofficial organizer of the events, and Valenti saw him talking briefly as Valenti found an unoccupied table and sat a little closer to the stage than he would have liked. O'Brian returned and seemed about to say something when the background sounds from the porno that was playing in one corner suddenly cut off and a hush fell over the room.

"Gentlemen and gentlemen." Peter was standing on the stage and waving his arms for attention. "You've all come to be entertained, and I can certainly promise you that. Our blowjob contest is about to start, so may I please have our blowers and blowees assembled on the stage."

Six men -- three sponsors and their twinks -- trooped up on stage, all wearing leather pants or shorts, and, in some cases, not much else. The sponsors stood with legs apart, flies down, and their twinks knelt before them, waiting for Peter to give the word. When the cheers and catcalls had died down and the room was absolutely silent, he did.

"Gentlemen, start your engines!" the little man yelled in a surprisingly loud voice. The "boys" on the floor had their sponsors out in record time, and soon three heads were bobbing at various rates of speed while the crowd in the back room of the Dark Knight cheered on their favorite teams.

Valenti found he couldn't look away from the action on the stage, although he desperately wanted to. The sight didn't do anything for him, but the thought that it could have been O'Brian and himself up there, with his partner on his knees before him, had his cock throbbing. He shifted uncomfortably in his chair, trying not to imagine O'Brian's mouth sliding over him, the hot, gentle suction as he took Valenti in...

"I can't not look." O'Brian leaned closer and whispered out of the corner of his mouth, planting a chaste kiss on Valenti's cheek as he spoke.

"I know -- it's like a train wreck," Valenti replied weakly, his eyes glued to the stage and his cock protesting vigorously in his pants. He stole a surreptitious glance at his partner's shorts to see if he was similarly affected and was slightly reassured to see the evidence of O'Brian's arousal pressing against the thin denim. So he wasn't the only one. He wondered why his partner was hard -- the excitement of the moment? The anticipation of performing for the crowd? Or just nerves? Sometimes he thought O'Brian got a hard-on the way other people got the hiccups or stuttered -- as a nervous reaction to certain situations.

The contest ended abruptly when one of the twinks pulled back, grinning, the evidence of his victory still in his mouth.

"What's the matter with you -- didn't your mother teach you never to talk with your mouth full?" Peter scolded him. The boy swallowed as obviously as possible, licking his lips for added effect, and the crowd went wild. "Team two, claim your prize," Peter said. He handed each of the winning contestants white T-shirts with black lettering and urged the men to show them off to the crowd. One read "I got blown at the RamJack," and the other read "I'm a sucker for the RamJack."

"Geeze, pretty cheesy," O'Brian commented, reading the shirts.

"Just watch yourself, partner, or you're liable to get one like it. Maybe it'll say, 'Wankathon Winner,' or 'Number One Wanker,' something classy like that. You can wear it to the next O'Brian family reunion. Should be a real conversation piece," Valenti whispered back, grinning, feeling more at ease when he could joke with his partner.

"Yeah, yeah, keep talkin', babe. I'm gonna show you how it's done." O'Brian squeezed Valenti's knee, an intimate gesture that brought his cock back to life harder than ever.

"All right now, gentlemen, that was just the beginning. For our next event, may I present to you a RamJack tradition -- the Wankathon!" Peter's voice rang out over the buzz of the crowd, and O'Brian got to his feet, rubbing the bulge in his shorts reflexively. "Will the wankers and the wankees please come to the stage." Peter continued.

"The...what?" Valenti could only stare as a new group of men filed onto the stage, O'Brian among them.

"Ah, we appear to have an odd number here, gentlemen." Peter was looking over the men on the stage. "We can't have that, now, can we? Young man..." He gestured for O'Brian, who came obligingly forward. "Will your sponsor be performing with you, or will you have a substitute wanker?"

"Uh..." O'Brian looked as close to panicked as Valenti had ever seen him.

"I'll do it!" It was the voice of Harry, the Neanderthal, and Valenti saw the involuntary tic of his partner's facial muscles as the huge man began to wade through the seats nearest the stage. O'Brian's green eyes were huge, and his normally tan face was pale as paper.

"That won't be necessary," Valenti heard himself saying. Rising to his feet, he made his way to the stage, vowing that he would kill O'Brian for getting them into this in the first place. "I'll do it," he said, reaching his partner's side and laying a possessive hand on O'Brian's arm. He could feel the tension thrumming through the compact frame, and he knew his friend was drawn as tight as a wire.

"Sorry, Valenti. Had no idea," O'Brian muttered out of the corner of his mouth.

"Neither one of us did. But I think it's too late to back out now," Valenti whispered back. The lights pointed at the stage were hot. Now that he was up on it, he realized he was sweating freely. There was a loud buzzing sound in his ears that must have been Peter talking because Valenti could see his mouth moving. But nothing the tiny man was saying was registering as words. He saw the other contestants begin to get into position and suddenly had to fight the panic that wanted to crawl up the back of his throat like bile.

"What the hell are we supposed to be doing, anyway?" he whispered desperately to O'Brian.

"Uh, I think you're s'posed to jerk me off." His partner already had his shorts unzipped and was standing with strong legs braced apart and his heavy shaft in one hand. *Trying to make it easy for me*, Valenti thought and was grateful. If he'd had to unzip O'Brian himself and then fumble around in the confines of those tight shorts for his partner's dick...well, the stage fright was already bad enough. At least all he had to do was step up behind O'Brian as he saw the other sponsors doing behind their boys and take his friend's cock in his hand.

Listen to me -- "that's all I have to do"? Once again he had the sensation that his universe was turning inside out. He'd never handled another man before, and now he was expected to manipulate his partner to orgasm, and in front of a crowd, no less. It was all so surreal.

"Not sure I can do this, Sean," he muttered in his partner's ear, feeling a trickle of cold sweat run down the groove of his spine like an icy finger.

"You got no choice, babe -- this could make or break us. Here." Valenti felt a strong hand close on his wrist and pull his arm down and around O'Brian's body. Then he felt the hard column of warm flesh brushing his palm. He grasped it automatically, a part of his brain registering how similar and yet how different it was from his own. "That's it," O'Brian whispered, and Valenti felt his partner back up against him so that the round, tight ass was pressed against his groin. "Now touch me, babe. Need to feel you touch me."

The words, spoken in a low, intense voice, seemed to have a magical effect on Valenti. This was his partner -- the man he loved -- and this might be the only time he would ever be able to show his love physically. He closed his eyes and leaned close to O'Brian's compact frame, burying his face in the warm, reddish-gold hair and breathing in the delicious, masculine scent of his friend, shutting out the bright lights and the randy, shouting crowd around the base of the stage.

He could feel O'Brian already rotating against him, pumping against the loose circle of his fingers, and he suddenly wanted to make this moment something neither of them ever forgot. Even after they went back to being platonic friends and co-workers out in the real world, he wanted O'Brian to remember the touch of his partner's hand holding him intimately, bringing him pleasure.

"Stop," Valenti growled, tightening his grip on his partner's shaft to still the pumping of those hips. O'Brian ground to a halt suddenly, stiffening against him, his whole body asking the question.

"Wanna touch you," Valenti muttered hoarsely in his ear. "Wanna make you feel good, Sean." He wound his other arm around his partner's chest so he could feel the heave and gasp of O'Brian's excited breathing and took a better grip on the thick cock in his hand.

Deliberately, he stroked from the base of his partner's shaft to the leaking tip of the broad head, the tender nugget of flesh left bare and vulnerable by circumcision. He thought he could feel the tiny scar, a little rougher than the rest of the steel-velvet shaft, just under the head. He caressed it with his thumb, spreading the slippery fluid over it and loving the slight difference in texture -- learning his partner as he had never been able to before and would never be able to again.

He heard O'Brian groan in his ear as the golden head leaned back against his shoulder for support, and felt the fine trembling of the other man's body against his as he made his leisurely exploration. He reached down to cup the tender sac, fondling and rolling the balls inside before taking another long, slow stroke over the straining shaft.

"For God's sake, Valenti... Driving me crazy!" O'Brian gasped in his ear, his entire body shaking with the barely contained urge to move, the need to thrust.

"Love you, partner," Valenti heard himself whisper, not even sure if O'Brian heard him. "Love you so much. Want to make you come."

"Do it... *Do it!*" O'Brian was panting heavily now, his chest pumping like a bellows under the restraining arm, and Valenti was happy to oblige him. He started a slow, sure stroke, caressing his partner's cock as he would his own, giving O'Brian permission to move, to meet the tempo Valenti was creating and match his rhythm.

He felt O'Brian's hips and ass undulating against his groin and realized that he was achingly hard himself. The feel of his partner's cock in his hand seemed to create a closed loop of pleasure between them, stoking the fire Valenti felt inside higher and higher until he thought it must consume him. He stroked long and firm, but faster now, and O'Brian thrust to meet him, offering his body as he had the night before, pressed trembling into the loving circle of Valenti's hand, trusting and vulnerable and so *hot*.

Valenti had never felt such emotion -- such longing and need and love and lust rolled up together until he thought his heart would explode with the unbearable mixture. There was no one else in the room but him and O'Brian, no one but this man leaning back against him to receive the pleasure Valenti gave, moving so naturally to the rhythm they had created together. This man he loved with his entire being. Valenti had a sudden urge to drop to his knees and take O'Brian's thick shaft into his mouth and down his throat, to suck instead of stroke, to catch the burning cum on his tongue instead of in his palm. But there was no time.

"Ah... God! VALENTI!" O'Brian shouted, and then Valenti felt the rhythmic spurts as the shaft in his hand released suddenly, coating his palm with sticky warmth, letting go of the incredible tension, the overwhelming need. Then his partner was sagging against him, clearly weak in the knees from the force of his orgasm. "Ah, babe..." O'Brian whispered, his voice ragged and low. "So good...so...*good.*" His heart was still pounding like a jackhammer under Valenti's palm.

Without thinking, Valenti reached around and turned O'Brian's face toward him and kissed his partner long and slow on those full, panting lips, even as the other man's shaft softened in his hand.

"Team three, if you are quite finished?" The voice of Peter broke the trance they were in.

Valenti broke the kiss reluctantly and looked up to see that every eye in the place was trained on them. Even the other contestants were standing quietly by, having obviously finished earlier. The room was silent; he and O'Brian were the sole focus of attention, and Valenti suddenly felt his stage fright come back full force, clawing at his throat with nervous fingers.

"Um...yeah. We're done," he mumbled, trying desperately to stuff O'Brian's semi-erect shaft back into the tight shorts, which didn't want to cooperate. How the hell did his partner manage in these things, anyway? To his great relief, O'Brian came to life and took over the operation at hand, tucking himself neatly away and standing up straight so that Valenti no longer had to support his weight.

"Gentlemen, I think I speak for all of us when I say, that was *beautiful.* Just an outstanding performance." The look on Peter's face was thoroughly gratified, and there were murmurs of agreement from the audience, and the other contestants, as well. "I think I have to award both the longest jerk and the best technique to this lovely, mismatched pair," he continued, and there were roars of approval from every side. Valenti felt like his whole body was blushing in shame. The weight of what he had done fell on him like a lead ball, and he just wanted to get off the stage.

"Thanks," he muttered. "Come on, Sean." He motioned for O'Brian to follow him and beat a hasty retreat down the side of the stage, pushing through the crowd and straight out past the leather curtain. The dim room outside seemed closer than ever, a claustrophobe's nightmare, and suddenly Valenti felt as though the weight of the entire RamJack was pressing down on his neck. He *had* to get out of the Basement.

Nearly running, ignoring the questioning look of the black-haired guard, he made his way out of the stone enclosure, through the black door, and up the narrow stairs. He heard footsteps running to catch up with him and knew O'Brian must be right behind, so that was all right. But he couldn't stop for anything until he got all the way out.

Finally he ground to a halt, gasping more with emotion than exertion at the top of the stairs, leaning with his fists pressed against his knees and his head hanging down. He could hear his heart thundering in his ears, and a cold sweat had broken out all over his body.

"Hey, babe...hey..." It was O'Brian's voice, and a warm hand on the back of his neck made Valenti look up briefly to see concern written large over the familiar face of his partner before he squeezed his eyes closed again. "C'mon, why don't you sit a minute? Make you feel better to take a load off," the voice continued reasonably. Valenti found himself being turned awkwardly, and a gentle pressure on his shoulders urged him down.

He didn't sit so much as collapse onto the top stair, head down and hands dangling between his knees. He realized that one palm was still sticky with his partner's cum, and he wiped it carefully on his shirt, over his heart.

"Okay," he muttered, not sure if he was trying to convince O'Brian or himself. "I'm okay." The blind panic was beginning to leave him, a cold dread taking its place. He looked up, but found he couldn't meet those sea-green eyes. "Sean," he said at last, sighing deeply. "Sean, I'm so damn sorry."

"What for?" There was genuine bewilderment in his partner's tone, and Valenti was surprised to see O'Brian peering at him with a worried frown. "You did what you had to do, Nick. We both did."

"But I shouldn't have made such a...such a production of it." Valenti didn't know how to explain what he really felt, the real reason he was sick and dizzy with dread. The act they had been required to perform could have been very mechanical -- almost clinical, if he had gone about it the right way. Instead, Valenti had let his feelings for his partner overcome him, had made it an act of intimacy -- an expression of his love. "Shouldn't have *enjoyed* it so much," he whispered.

"Hey, I enjoyed it, too, ya big dummy. Or didn't you notice?" O'Brian grinned at him, seemingly unaffected. "What's wrong with you, anyway?"

"What's *wrong* with me?" Valenti looked at his partner in disbelief, and O'Brian looked innocently back. "I just jerked you off, Sean -- in front of a crowded room. We've been kissing and groping all over each other since we got here. Last night I...you..." He couldn't find the words to complete his thought. "This is going to *change* us, partner," he said at last. "There's no way it can't."

"What are you talking about, Nicky? Change us how? We're undercover -- we do what we have to. Why do you have to take everything so seriously? Why does everything always have to be a federal case with you?"

Valenti just looked at him in weary disbelief. The earth had moved for him, but his partner hadn't felt so much as a tremor. It was too much. He stood shakily to his feet.

"Hey, where ya goin'?" O'Brian asked anxiously, rising beside him and taking his arm.

Valenti shook him off. "I don't know. Away. Back to the room." He shambled heavily down the polished wood hallway, not bothering to glance at the posh beauty around him. He felt wrung out -- beaten. This was all a job to O'Brian; nothing he could do or say would touch his partner's heart. His fear that O'Brian might be angry with him for making the contact between them such an intimate occasion now seemed entirely laughable.

"Hey...*hey*..." O'Brian called after him, but Valenti just kept on walking. There was nothing left to say.

Chapter Ten

Dinner that night was a silent affair. Valenti wouldn't have attended at all if they hadn't been on assignment. His mind and every part of his body felt heavy and dull, and he heard O'Brian explain several times that his partner wasn't quite feeling himself. Word of the Wankathon had spread, and they were congratulated several times on their "outstanding performance." Valenti was dimly aware that his partner was wearing a tight white T-shirt with the words "I Beat My Meat at the RamJack" across the front, but he found he just couldn't be interested.

After returning to the room, he had lain facedown on the bed for hours, trying to think -- trying to make sense of it all. Once or twice it had seemed that maybe O'Brian might actually return his feelings. Valenti thought of the tender way his partner had washed his belly and thighs the night before -- the hot suction of O'Brian's mouth on the head of his cock. And what about the kiss they had shared before leaving the room this afternoon? The way O'Brian had verbalized his love, something Valenti knew wasn't easy for his friend, no matter how much he might feel it. But what *kind* of love?

O'Brian had jumped into this assignment with both feet and taken to his role as Valenti's lover as though it was the most natural thing in the world. Last night he had even initiated physical intimacy between them without the benefit of an audience for an excuse. But despite all the touching and kissing going on between them, O'Brian still seemed essentially unmoved.

Valenti had seen his partner when he was in love with a woman, and he wasn't acting that way at all. He was just behaving normally -- the way he always acted around his partner. Valenti had no choice but to assume that it was all in a day's work for his friend and that O'Brian really was unmoved by the physical contact between them. He admitted to himself that his partner would probably be just as happy when they finished this assignment and could go back to their old routine -- a platonic friendship with casual, nonsexual touching.

Valenti didn't know if he could stand it. The whole situation was getting to him. To be able to touch his partner any way he wanted and yet know there was no way he could touch O'Brian's heart... It was devastatingly hurtful. He wondered for the millionth time how he could ever have been so stupid as to let himself fall in love with the one person who was more important to him than anyone else. And yet -- how could he have prevented it?

There were no easy answers. After dinner, he let O'Brian lead him back to the room, making excuses along the way to Paul and Remy, who had invited them up to their room for a rousing game of strip Canasta.

"Maybe tomorrow night. Charles isn't feeling so well right now," he heard his partner say. "But I'll meet you tomorrow before breakfast to talk about what we discussed, Remy."

"See ya'll later, then," was the soft reply. And then, much to Valenti's relief, they were stepping into their room, and O'Brian was locking the door behind them.

"C'mon, Valenti, you've been in a funk all night," O'Brian said, leading him toward the bathroom. "Let's see if a little soap and water can make things better."

Valenti wanted to say that nothing would ever be better again, but it seemed like too much effort to get the words out. He had felt like this after Madeline had left him, and O'Brian had pulled him through. But tonight his partner was the cause of his depression, so he didn't see how anything O'Brian could do would help.

"Ya know, you're a moody son of a bitch," O'Brian remarked as he started to strip off Valenti's clothes, folding them neatly on the counter as he went. "Don't know why I love you so much."

It was the second time in twenty-four hours his partner had said that he loved him, but Valenti knew better than to get too excited. He knew what O'Brian was really saying was, "You're my best friend in the whole world," not, "Here's my heart, take it, it's yours." He stood pliant, not caring what happened, while O'Brian stripped them both down to the skin and turned on the shower, letting the steam rise as the water got hot.

"C'mon, Nicky, into the shower." O'Brian pushed him in and then, somewhat to Valenti's surprise, followed after him. He supposed his partner was just "staying in character," and didn't comment.

The showerhead was a broad one, and it was spraying powerfully enough for them both to get wet at once. Valenti closed his eyes, stood still, and let the water, which was just this side of too hot, thunder over his skull and run in rivulets down his back and chest. After a moment he felt an unfamiliar sensation and realized that O'Brian was scrubbing his back with a soapy washcloth. He opened his mouth, and at last words came out.

"You don't have to do that, you know. It's a bit above and beyond the call of duty, don't you think?" He meant the words to come out sarcastic, but they just sounded tired.

"Ah-ha -- it speaks," O'Brian said, apparently unperturbed. He transferred his attention from Valenti's back to his sides and chest. "Love how smooth you are," O'Brian whispered, scrubbing carefully between the flat, coppery disks of Valenti's nipples. "Not like me. 'M such a hairball."

"I like your hair," Valenti said, reaching up to run one searching finger through the dripping mat of reddish-gold curls on his partner's chest. O'Brian shivered noticeably under his touch.

"I'm sorry this assignment has been so hard on you, partner," O'Brian said at last, when Valenti thought he wasn't going to answer. Sea-green eyes looked up from under dripping gold lashes, and Valenti thought his partner had never looked more beautiful or more unobtainable. "I never should've dragged us into this. It's hurtin' you, bein' here; I can see that now. I never meant for it to hurt you, Nick." The washcloth moved lower, swiping over his legs, but Valenti barely felt it.

"It's not your fault, Sean," he said, not wishing to cause his friend pain. "It's just…difficult circumstances."

"I know." A pause, and then O'Brian said in a voice that was almost too low to hear over the gush of the water, "I'm sorry it was so hard for you to touch me."

Valenti, who had closed his eyes and turned his face toward the water, turned back to face his partner, surprised.

"I mean, that's why you ran out of there so fast, huh?" O'Brian said, not looking at him.

"No." Valenti tried to think of a way to refute the claim without letting go of his own secret. How ironic that his partner thought Valenti didn't want to touch him, when the exact opposite was true. *I could spend the rest of my life touching you…making you come…loving you.*

He thought about his childhood -- loveless, barren, devoid of physical affection. It was O'Brian who had taught him how to touch in the first place, how to take pleasure in the simple, human warmth of a handshake, a neck rub, a hug, the feeling of your partner's thigh pressed alongside your own as you sat on the couch and watched the game on TV.

It wasn't O'Brian's fault that Valenti had taken his gift and perverted it, that he had come to crave more than he had any right to expect O'Brian to give under normal circumstances. Except that here at the RamJack, circumstances were anything but normal. *Why can't I just enjoy this time with him while I've got it?* It was a golden opportunity, and he was pissing it away.

"Sean," he said at last. "It wasn't like that. I just...I got nervous thinking about all those guys watching us. And I thought you'd be upset because...because of the way I touched you." He laughed a little at himself and shook his head. "I realize now that was silly of me."

"Damn straight," O'Brian said without a trace of irony, and then he was in Valenti's arms, melting against him, pressing the way he had that night on the dance floor of the Dancing Queen.

Valenti felt his cock stand to attention, throbbing and angry -- unfulfilled. O'Brian's rose to join it, and that perfect friction he remembered from the night before began a slow fire in his belly as the water ran over them and his partner kissed him fiercely on the mouth. At last he drew away, feeling breathless.

"Sean, you don't have to do this." He rubbed wet circles over his partner's back with gentle fingers.

"Don't have to, but I want to. Wanna take care of you tonight. C'mon." O'Brian pulled away and turned off the shower, reaching for towels for them both. He dried himself briskly and then Valenti, as well; he seemed to think his partner was moving too slowly. "Come in the bedroom, babe. I want to make you feel good."

"You don't have to," Valenti said again as O'Brian laid him facedown on the bed and dimmed the lights so that only a dark silhouette was beside him in the shadow. Strong hands began to massage his back, easing away the physical tension. Valenti sighed blissfully. O'Brian always gave the best backrubs, although he had never done it sans clothing before.

The thought of his partner kneeling over him, of that lithe, naked body with its mat of crisp, golden-red hair behind him, touching him, made his cock throb uselessly against the bed. Valenti shifted, trying to get more comfortable. He supposed O'Brian was doing this as an act of friendship, a gesture of reconciliation for the disagreement they'd had earlier. *Might as well enjoy the naked massages while you can get them, Nicholas. This is a one-time-only deal -- good exclusively at the RamJack.*

Warm. O'Brian's hands were so *warm*. Masculine and capable, kneading against his spine and down over his buttocks and thighs. Valenti gave himself up to the pleasure of being touched and tried to forget the throbbing of his cock. O'Brian might not love Valenti the way Valenti loved him, might not return his passion, but it was still comforting to have the other man so close, touching him this way. He could feel himself melting, relaxing under those hands...

A warm wetness at the top of his left thigh took him by surprise. Valenti jerked and turned his head away from the pillow it had been resting on. Feeling the sensation again, higher up, he realized O'Brian was kissing him.

"Wha...?" he began, and then he felt O'Brian parting his thighs, and a hot tongue was bathing his balls from behind. "Oh, God, Sean...you don't...you shouldn't..." he protested as the ticklish warm wetness went on and on, making him want to squirm and hold rigidly still at the same time for fear of interrupting the intense pleasure.

"Turn over." His partner's voice was low and commanding. Valenti found himself rolling over onto his back, his cock an angry exclamation point in the darkness, jutting up from between his thighs. A hand cupped him, soothing the ache with a steady stroke.

"Sean..." he protested, wishing he could see the expression on the other man's face.

"We're partners. Partners take care of each other," O'Brian whispered in the darkness, his hand caressing, exploring, claiming.

"That's no reason to do… Ah! Things you wouldn't normally want to do," Valenti admonished him. He was thrusting into that warm, firm grip now. He could feel the calluses on O'Brian's palm from gripping his gun. It was so different from the soft, smooth palm of a woman, so unlike any hand-job he had ever gotten, and a hundred times better because it was his partner doing the stroking. He heard a short chuff of laughter in the darkness.

"Since when is anything normal lately?" O'Brian asked. "Nick, the way you touched me today… I don't know. It was beautiful. I just want to give a little of that back."

"There's…no obligation." Valenti panted, although he thought he might die of blue balls if his partner stopped now. "Did it…because I wanted to."

"And I want to do this." The blond head lowered suddenly, and Valenti was enveloped in a wet, glorious heat down to his root. It was obviously a move O'Brian had never performed before because he pulled back quickly, gagging a little. But he didn't stop. Valenti felt a profusion of golden hair brushing under his palms as he reached down -- to stop his partner or to urge him on, he wasn't sure which.

"Sean, no…no, don't…" The blond head lifted for a moment, but Valenti could feel his partner's hot breath blowing across the sensitive skin of his cock as O'Brian spoke.

"Just wanna do this for you tonight, Nick. Please, babe, let me give you this. Let me taste you." Without waiting for a reply, he lowered his head and engulfed Valenti's cock again, sucking and stroking at the same time as Valenti shivered and gasped beneath his mouth.

"Oh, God, Sean…" Valenti groaned, unable to express the pleasure he was feeling.

How many times had a woman done this for him? And yet now, as O'Brian sucked and lapped, twisting his hot tongue experimentally around Valenti's throbbing shaft and then taking it all in his mouth, it was like the first time. He felt a gentle hand reach between his legs to cup his balls tenderly as the warm, wet suction went on and on, and he moaned aloud at the added sensation.

O'Brian lapped at the broad head, exploring the slit with the tip of his tongue, and then swallowed Valenti's aching shaft down to the root again, sucking strongly. Valenti would have bet any amount of money that O'Brian had never given a blowjob before, had never taken another man's cock in his mouth, so how in the hell could his partner be so good at it?

"How...?" he gasped, unable to form a coherent question. O'Brian understood.

"Just doin'...what feels good...to me," he whispered, stroking slowly along the aching shaft and leaving hot, open-mouthed kisses in a trail down to Valenti's balls as he spoke. "'S all right?"

"More than all right." Valenti thrust reflexively as the blond head began bobbing against his groin once more, pulling his cock into that warm, wet suction. "You don't stop...I'm gonna come."

He expected O'Brian to pull back and finish him off with his hand, but instead his partner mumbled, "Want you to. Want to taste you, babe. Come for me." O'Brian's mouth engulfed him again and began a steady rhythm that Valenti couldn't possibly resist.

His fingers clenched in the sheets and his hips bucked helplessly as O'Brian continued to suck him relentlessly toward the edge of orgasm. He still had no idea why his partner was doing this for him, but he couldn't care anymore. His whole consciousness was centered on his groin -- completely taken up with the sensations of O'Brian's mouth doing incredible things, things he had never even believed possible.

He didn't know if this was the best blowjob he had ever received, or if it was just phenomenal because it was O'Brian doing the sucking. It had been so long since he had experienced sex and love at the same time, it was hard to tell.

One of O'Brian's hands was stroking and fondling his balls, using feather-light touches that seemed to set all his nerve endings on fire as the slippery warmth on his cock went on and on. Suddenly it was too much, and Valenti felt himself tilting over the edge.

"Oh, God, Sean...gonna..." He couldn't finish the thought. He felt himself thrusting up hard, unable to resist as his partner leaned forward to take him as deep as possible into that warm, willing throat. Hot spurts jetted out of his cock over and over as the pleasure crested inside, and he could feel O'Brian swallowing steadily, taking everything Valenti had to give and sucking gently to get more. At last he felt himself coming down, felt his cock beginning to lose its aching rigidity, and with a final, soft kiss to the broad head, O'Brian released him.

"C'mere," Valenti managed to mumble. He was glad to feel the golden head resting on his shoulder a moment later and his partner nuzzling close against his side. "That was...incredible," he whispered into the soft, fragrant hair. The compact frame fit perfectly against his own, and O'Brian smelled like clean sweat and sexual musk -- delicious. "You didn't have to do it, though. Would you like...?" He reached down for O'Brian's groin, but a gentle hand pushed him firmly away.

"Better be careful, or you'll get a handful of cum, babe." O'Brian's voice was low and amused. "I came like a rocket right behind you when I felt you shoot down my throat. You taste delicious, didja know that?"

"Madeline never cared much for it. What's it like?" Valenti asked, meaning the whole experience. "I've never...I don't know...tasted anyone else's."

O'Brian understood. "Well, it's a little weird at first. It's something I've had done to me a lot but never expected to do to anybody else, ya know? It was different, but not bad. Don't get me wrong, though, Nick -- you're the only guy I'd ever do it for." O'Brian shifted against him and rubbed Valenti's belly soothingly. "Now, why don'tcha try to get some sleep? I've got a meeting with Remy tomorrow mornin', and I think we're finally gonna score. Gonna be outta this freak show before you know it."

His words made Valenti unaccountably sad. Of course he knew that O'Brian would be happy to get away from here and get back to their normal routine. He didn't harbor any illusions that what his partner had done for him tonight was anything more than a one-time deal. It was an expression of friendship, not love. He knew all of it in his head, and yet his heart couldn't help feeling sore and tired all over again.

"Love you, Sean," he whispered into the soft blond hair. "You're the best partner, best friend anybody could ever ask for. What you've done for me while we've been here, well, I'll never forget it." His partner grew very still for a moment in his arms, and then Valenti heard a low, heavy sigh.

"Yeah, back at ya, babe," O'Brian whispered finally. "Look, I'm gonna get cleaned up now and then turn in. Gotta get up early for my little meeting tomorrow. You just take it easy." He started to pull out of the circle of Valenti's arms, but Valenti couldn't stand to let him go just yet.

"Wait, Sean..." He held on to his partner, hesitating, and then thought, *What the hell.* "Could I...I just want one more kiss. To taste..." He couldn't finish the thought out loud, couldn't say that he wanted to taste himself on his partner's lips, in that hot, wet mouth. He felt O'Brian tremble against him.

"'Course you c'n have a kiss, Nick," O'Brian whispered. Then he was leaning over, a darker shape in the darkness. Valenti could again smell the mixture of spicy musk and clean sweat that was entirely O'Brian. Then his partner bent down and took his mouth, so sweetly and completely that everything else but the kiss was driven out of his mind.

O'Brian's tongue probed deeply, giving Valenti back the flavor of himself, salty and slightly bitter -- a taste that reminded him of tears. His hand crept up and tangled in the soft nest of his partner's hair, holding O'Brian close for just a moment more. Never wanting to let him go.

"You taste like the ocean," O'Brian murmured when they parted at last.

"Sean, I..." It was on the tip of his tongue to admit everything, to let his partner know once and for all how he really felt. But why make it harder than it already was? O'Brian had given him a wonderful gift -- the gift of himself. Valenti knew he couldn't be so selfish as to demand that the gift continue once they left this place. But at least he would always have the memories to treasure.

"Yeah? Talk to me, Nick." O'Brian's voice was tense, somehow yearning in the dark. Valenti wondered what his partner wanted him to say. He wished he knew, because he couldn't say what was really in his heart.

"Nothing," he said at last. "Just that I'll never forget this -- our time here, I mean. Even when we get out of here and everything's...back to normal."

Another heavy sigh, and then O'Brian was sliding off the bed. "Yeah, me neither, Nicky. Me neither."

By the time his partner came back to bed, Valenti was already asleep. And when he woke up, O'Brian was gone.

Chapter Eleven

He wasn't too worried at first. O'Brian had turned off the alarm clock to let him sleep late. It was just one of those small things they did for each other -- little gestures of caring that Valenti had come to take for granted over the years.

Now, he wondered, as he rolled over and saw that it was nearly ten, how he could ever have taken anything his partner did for him as a matter of course. All the little touches, the small comforts they shared together -- he had never had them with anyone else. Not with Madeline, even though they had been really close right before she left.

Near the end of his marriage to Madeline, she had refused to touch him at all, and that had been very hard. There was a deep well of longing in Valenti to touch and be touched, and when Madeline had left him aching and empty, O'Brian had filled the void.

Valenti would never forget the night after the divorce was final...

O'Brian drove him home, and Valenti said goodnight and trudged up the steps to his apartment -- an apartment that felt so empty and wrong without Madeline. He heard footsteps behind him, and looking back, he saw, to his surprise, that O'Brian was following him.

His partner had never just invited himself in before, but that night he didn't even ask. Just waited while Valenti unlocked the door and then walked into the living room as though it was something he did every night. O'Brian went to the couch and sat, looking expectantly at Valenti, who stared back dully.

"What?" Valenti didn't have a clue what O'Brian was up to, and he was pretty much too tired and emotionally drained to care.

"C'mere," his partner replied, patting the couch beside him.

"Why?" Valenti felt the obligation to ask.

"Just c'mere," was O'Brian's reply. Valenti went to him, too tired to fight about it, and sat where his partner indicated. Without speaking another word, O'Brian wrapped his arms around Valenti and pulled him close.

"What...?" Valenti tried to protest, but the feeling of strong arms around him -- the wonderful sensation of being held close to the one person in the world who would kill or die for him, who would never let him go -- was too strong to resist. Sighing heavily, he allowed himself to relax against O'Brian, wrapped his arms around the trim waist, and closed his eyes.

They sat like that for most of an hour, not saying anything. Valenti hadn't wept then; the pain had been too deep for tears. But the feeling of his friend's hands carding gently through his hair and the comforting scratch of O'Brian's chest hair against his cheek had been like water to a man dying of thirst.

It was a well that never ran dry, and O'Brian never seemed to mind how often he came to drink from it. Words didn't even seem to be necessary between them; somehow his partner just knew when he needed to be touched...

Was that when I started to love him? Even before I almost lost him to the point of a junkie's knife?

Valenti shook his head and went for the shower. He remembered how gently O'Brian had washed him the night before and the way he had taken care of Valenti afterwards. He hadn't had to tell O'Brian what he needed; his partner had just known and provided it as he always did.

If only this assignment could go on forever, if only they didn't have to go back to being what they had always been when it was over -- the best of friends, but still *just* friends. *Ah, Sean, we could be everything to each other. I don't need anyone else when I'm with you.*

If only they could keep the physical aspect of their relationship that they had discovered at the RamJack. But Valenti knew it was impossible. O'Brian might be willing to play gay undercover and even push his personal boundaries enough to fulfill the unspoken fantasies of his partner once or twice. But it couldn't last on the outside. There were too many pretty girls in short skirts in the world, and Valenti had no illusions as to where his partner's true preferences lay. He couldn't ask O'Brian to give up the pleasures of a woman's soft body for a committed sexual relationship with his partner.

O'Brian loved Valenti very much; he was sure of that. But his partner wasn't *in love*. Valenti, on the other hand, was deeply in love, in want, in need, and he saw no way out. For the first time, he began to wonder if it might be better for him to leave O'Brian in peace when this assignment was over. After six wonderful years of partnership and a friendship unlike any other he had ever had, maybe it was time to move on.

After drying off and getting dressed, Valenti glanced at the clock and realized it was almost eleven. He began to be alarmed. O'Brian had seemed very sure of himself when he talked about "dealing," and Valenti had assumed that he would probably use Remy to convince Conrad to sell them some coke. Once the deal was done, the bust could happen, although he was sure O'Brian would have informed him of it by now.

He began to get a bad feeling in the pit of his stomach. He should have heard from his partner by now. He shouldn't have slept in and taken such a leisurely shower, letting himself brood over things he had no control over while his partner was doing the deal. He needed to be out there with O'Brian, getting his back instead of sulking like a child.

Hurriedly, he pulled on some clothes and went for the door. As he pulled open its solid oak surface, he came face to face with the same two goons who had delivered O'Brian to the door on the day they had first come to the RamJack. But this time his partner was nowhere to be seen.

"What --?" Valenti started to ask, but he was grabbed roughly under both arms before he could complete the question. His shoes barely touched the floor as he was dragged forcefully down the carpeted hall. He tried to struggle, but it was useless, like fighting a brick wall.

"Take it easy there, *Detective*," the black- haired security guard who had taunted O'Brian the day before growled in his gravely voice. "Wouldn't wanna get yourself all messed up before the show, now, would ya?" Valenti felt himself sag in their grip. Detective. So the jig was up, their cover blown. Only one question mattered now.

"Where's my partner?" he asked, hoping against hope that O'Brian had somehow escaped, although he knew his friend wouldn't leave without him.

"Oh, he's *real* comfortable; don't worry about that. He's waiting for you right now, as a matter of fact," Thad, the blond, answered. His side-of-beef face was twisted into a nasty sneer that seemed to stop Valenti's heart in his chest.

"Where are you taking me?" he asked at last. Wherever it was, as long as he and O'Brian would be together, maybe they could figure something out.

"The Viewing Room," Thad answered briefly, and that was all he could get out of them.

Chapter Twelve

Valenti tried to still the pounding of his heart as he was dragged down the darks steps leading to the Basement and re-entered the claustrophobic confines of the ominous stone walls. He heard nothing but the echo of their footsteps and the gasp of his own breathing in his ears. Not even the distant throb of music greeted him as they passed through the farthest stone arch labeled THE VIEWING ROOM and pressed deeper into the bowels of the labyrinth beneath the RamJack.

Valenti wondered distractedly if all the other guests were somewhere else, or if the walls were simply too thick to hear the noise of the continuous partying. But mainly his thoughts were with his partner.

Where are you, Sean? What have they done to you? Twonnie's story about the fate of the rival drug thugs who had tried to penetrate the RamJack kept echoing in his head. *I swear to God, if they've so much as touched you that way...* He would kill them. He didn't know how, but he would, Valenti decided grimly.

At last, after what seemed like an eternity of hollow, stone corridors, they passed through another arching doorway and into a cavernous room that was set up like a theater. There were plush seats in rows leading down a slightly sloping floor and a stage placed in the middle of the room.

Mounted on the stage was a large glass box, and clearly visible inside was a bedroom set-up complete with a king-sized bed and night tables with ornate brass lamps on them. A Persian carpet covered the floor of the "bedroom," but it was the figure huddled in the middle of that vast expanse of mattress that drew Valenti's undivided attention.

"Sean…" he breathed, unable to help himself. In the center of the huge bed, curled in a fetal position with arms and legs bound, blindfolded and gagged, was his partner. O'Brian's helpless position was terrible to see, and the fact that he was completely naked fed Valenti's worst fears. "You bastards," he said thickly, struggling to be free of the punishing grip of the guards flanking him. "What have you done to him?"

"Nothing has been done to your partner as of yet, Detective Valenti." The smooth, cold voice came from one side of the glass box, and Valenti pulled his attention away from his partner long enough to see Conrad striding around the side of the stage, gray eyes flashing icily. "That pleasure had been reserved for you."

"What the hell are you talking about?" Valenti spat, wishing he could get his hands around that long, thin greyhound throat and smash the aristocratic knife-blade nose into Connor's brain. As an afterthought, he added, "How did you know?"

"About your little deception? Please, Detective, give me some credit. I have eyes and ears everywhere, especially in the law-enforcement community. I knew, when a batch of my…ah…*product* was incorrectly cut and resulted in some deaths, that someone was bound to come nosing around after me.

"It wasn't my fault, you understand. I would never harm my own community that way. It was the dealer I entrusted with that particular batch who made the mistake, but of course I was blamed. He was trying to, as they say, 'skim a little off the top.' Let me assure you that he will never make that particular mistake again." He grinned, a cold expression that never reached the gray eyes, and Valenti knew the dealer in question was already dead somewhere, rotting in an unmarked grave or shark-bait in the bay.

Conrad was a killer, no doubt about it, and they would be damn lucky to get out of here with their lives.

"So you blew our cover," he said as coolly as he could, trying not to let his eyes wander back to his partner bound helplessly on the bed. Every part of his being yearned to run to O'Brian and pull his friend into his arms, to comfort and soothe and look over the lithe, compact body for signs of harm, but he couldn't let that show on his face. "Even you couldn't be so stupid as to kill a couple of cops, Conrad," he said, trying to gauge the reaction to his words in those dead gray eyes.

"Oh, certainly not. Most uncivilized, the murder of our boys in blue." Conrad nodded his head solicitously towards the stage. "I wish only to teach you a lesson that you will not soon forget."

Valenti's heart pounded against his ribs; he could guess what kind of lesson Conrad had in mind.

"Now, Detective Valenti, you look positively pale, which is no mean feat for a man of your handsome complexion." The thin lips twitched into a smile that promised many things, all of them excruciatingly unpleasant. "I assume from the expression on your face that you have heard of my usual methods of persuasion."

Valenti only nodded, not trusting his voice. Conrad had descended the stage now and was circling around him, but not too close. The man had to know that if the goons on either side let go of Valenti, he would be on Conrad in a New York minute, but he obviously wanted to be close enough to gloat.

"I considered the...ah...usual treatment, Detective." Conrad grinned, circling like a shark. "But then I had a stroke of, well, I suppose I must call it genius. Not that I am vain, you understand." He smiled modestly, one hand placed on his slender chest. He was wearing a suit that was ice-cream white, and his olive skin stood out with sallow perfection against its creamy fabric. Valenti was silent, watching, waiting.

"You see," Conrad continued, coming to a halt in front of Valenti, "you are correct in assuming that I dare not kill you. No matter how secretly or skillfully it was done, I am afraid such an act would come back to haunt me. No, what I need from you is simply your silence. Your willingness to go back to where you came from, like good little boys, and never bother me again."

"Not going to happen," Valenti said stubbornly, meeting those dead eyes with his own, letting the certainty fill his face.

"Oh, but it will. I will make it happen. Or rather, *you*, Detective Valenti, will make it happen. What is the worst thing besides death that can happen to a red-blooded male like yourself?" He grinned lazily, letting the threat fill his thin face, and Valenti shivered involuntarily. *Rape. He's talking about rape.* He shook his head, refusing to give Conrad the satisfaction of an answer.

"I could order Thad and Brutus to take you and your partner right here and now," Conrad said, his voice flat and certain. He reached out and traced a line down Valenti's cheek with one long, thin finger. Valenti worked hard not to flinch from the icy touch. "And what a sight it would be, my two brutes covering you both. The delicious slap of flesh against flesh as they showed you the true meaning of submission. But I have conceived of a superior idea, a more diverting exhibition by far."

Valenti's blood ran cold, and he glanced involuntarily at his partner still curled in the center of the vast bed. What could be worse than being raped by Conrad's goons?

Conrad was watching him avidly and saw the quick glance toward O'Brian.

"You care for him deeply, do you not? Your partner?" He nodded over his shoulder at the stage. "But not in the way *we* care for each other. You are friends, partners, but not lovers. You are, as they say, 'straight,' no?"

There was a click in Valenti's throat as he answered, "Yes." No need to let Conrad know how far they had pushed the boundaries of their partnership these last few days at the RamJack.

"How difficult this little charade must have been for you, then." Conrad seemed most amused at the thought of their discomfort. "How uncomfortable to touch each other in such a *forbidden* way. I'll admit --" He chuckled. "-- that the kiss that you shared with him the first night almost convinced me. You are excellent actors, the both of you. And now you will be given the opportunity to put your considerable talent to use once more before you leave us here at the RamJack."

"What..." Valenti's mouth was dry. He swallowed convulsively. "What are you talking about, Conrad?" he asked. The gray shark-eyes looked coolly into his own.

"Blackmail, Detective. Of you and your partner. And security for myself. After this afternoon's show, neither of you will have any reason to ever bother me again. In fact, you will have ample reason not to. You see," he continued, reaching out once more to caress Valenti's cheek, "you and your partner are going to give a performance that you will not soon forget, and I will capture the whole of it on film. A film that will remain in my vault forever, unseen by anyone but myself unless you attempt to pry into my business again.

"That would be most unfortunate because the film could so easily be duplicated and circulated to anyone who had an interest. Newspapers, television stations, superior officers, and the like. Come." He motioned briskly to the guards.

Valenti found himself hauled up a short flight of steps and onto the stage. He could see O'Brian more clearly now. The bindings they had put around his partner's wrists and ankles were cruelly tight, and the blindfold he wore was black silk that stood out against the reddish-gold of his tousled hair.

"What are you expecting us to do?" Valenti asked, although he was terribly afraid he already knew the answer.

"Why, Detective Valenti, I thought that would be obvious. I expect you to fuck."

Chapter Thirteen

All the air seemed to leave his lungs at once at Conrad's words. Valenti just looked at him, hoping he had heard incorrectly, knowing he had not.

"Yes," Conrad continued. "You will fuck each other. Or rather, you, Detective Valenti, will fuck your partner. You kissed him so deliciously the other night that I find myself longing to see more. I have provided all the amenities; you need only to look in the drawer of the nightstand to find everything you need to...ah, ease your way. I will be recording your performance although you will not see me. Attempting to escape is useless; the glass is shatterproof, and there will be armed guards waiting at the entrance to the Viewing Room even if you should manage to break out of the box." He indicated the glass enclosure at center stage.

I'm supposed to fuck O'Brian? My best friend -- my partner? Valenti's mouth was dry with desire and self-hatred. The ultimate expression of his love. The ultimate betrayal.

"How..." He licked his lips nervously, trying to think how to phrase the question. "You said yourself we're straight, Conrad. We don't swing that way. How the hell do you expect me to get it up and do the job when that's the case?"

"You had better 'get it up,' as you say, Detective," Conrad said grimly. "Otherwise, at the end of a one-hour period, you will be forced to watch as Thad and Brutus take turns with your partner. I assure you, they are both most eager and will have no problem 'doing the job,' as you put it." A burst of trollish laughter from either side of him reminded Valenti of the two goons flanking him and reinforced Conrad's threat. "And then I will allow them to have a taste of your charms, as well," he continued, smiling coldly. "I assume that a forced union with your partner, however distasteful to you, will still be more agreeable than being left to the tender mercies of my guards. Am I correct?"

Valenti stared at him, refusing to answer, and Conrad finally shrugged. Producing a small key from the pocket of his cream-colored vest, he unlocked a glass panel that served as a door in the large box.

"Well, only time will tell. One hour, to be exact, gentlemen. After that, Thad and Brutus can have their fun. I assure you, it's immaterial to me which outcome I capture on film; either one will be sufficient to ensure your silence." Valenti was shoved rudely into the glass box, the backs of his knees hitting the bed where his partner lay. O'Brian stirred and moaned softly from behind the gag.

"How do we know you'll keep your word and let us go if we do what you say?" Valenti asked, suppressing the urge to go to his partner at once.

Conrad placed a slim, elegant hand over his heart. "Why, Detective Valenti, you wound me. It would be in the poorest taste to go back on my word as a gentleman once it has been given. There are certain things one does not do. Did you not notice how courteously I waited until you had gotten your full rest before having my men escort you down here?"

Valenti swallowed and closed his eyes briefly. So O'Brian had been lying here bound on the bed for hours while he lounged around in the luxurious suite upstairs, licking his wounds and feeling sorry for himself. Conrad's code of honor was a twisted thing indeed, but Valenti tended to feel he would be bound by it.

"Have you any further questions, Detective?" Conrad asked solicitously, as though they were at a cocktail party and he was asking if Valenti wanted another drink. "No? Then I leave you to your task. Let me warn you that I expect a good performance, which includes full penetration of your partner. I will know if you attempt to fake the act, and the consequences will be most dire. I *abhor* dishonesty. Good day, gentlemen." He withdrew, and there was a small snicking sound as the door closed and locked.

Valenti did the only thing he could do and turned toward the bed.

Chapter Fourteen

"Sean?" Valenti whispered softly, kneeling next to the bound man on the bed. Gently he loosened the gag from his partner's mouth and began to work on the knots that held his wrists and ankles. "You okay?" he asked, fumbling in his haste to get his partner untied.

"Knew..." O'Brian coughed harshly, his mouth obviously dried out by the gag. "Knew you'd come," he whispered hoarsely, turning blindly toward the sound of Valenti's voice.

"You may wish I hadn't in a while," Valenti said grimly, loosening the last knot so that O'Brian's arms and legs were free. His partner stretched gingerly and tried to sit up, but failed. "Hey, lie still while I get some circulation going again," Valenti ordered. He bent over his partner, massaging O'Brian's arms and legs until they began to regain color and feeling. "Son of a bitch, tying you up like that..."

"He's gonna do worse than tie me up if we don't figure a way out of this, Nicky," O'Brian said. "Here, I wanna..." He raised one hand to tug at the blindfold and hissed at the sudden invasion of light as the black silk came free. "Damn, that's bright!"

"Did...did you hear what he said?" Valenti asked, trying to keep his voice level. "About what --"

"Yeah, I heard," O'Brian interrupted him. He was up from the bed now, exploring the confines of their glass prison. From inside it, Valenti could see that it must be made of the same type of glass as a two-way mirror. Standing on the stage and looking at it, he had been able to see into the box. Now, from the inside, he could only see reflections of himself and his partner and the bedroom furniture. Nothing of the stage or the theater outside was visible. Even the ceiling was a mirror, reflecting his own worried expression back at him when he looked up.

"Bastard had me blindfolded and gagged, but he didn't do nothin' to my ears," O'Brian continued grimly. "S'pose he wanted me to hear what you were gonna have to do to me in detail."

"Sean, don't talk about it," Valenti begged, trying not to look at the many reflections of his partner's strong, naked form as O'Brian continued to prowl around the room, looking for a means of escape. He didn't dare admit to himself how much the hateful idea turned him on -- how much he wanted to feel that golden, compact body against his own, writhing beneath him...

"Nick, we may *have* to talk about it. I don't see an easy way outta here." O'Brian sat at last and gave him an unreadable look.

"No, I don't accept that!" Valenti turned from those fathomless green eyes and grabbed one of the heavy brass lamps from the nightstand nearest him. With all his strength he hurled the heavy lamp at the side of their mirrored prison. It bounced harmlessly off with an impotent clatter and came to rest at the foot of the bed, its bulb not even broken.

"Goddammit!" Valenti swore. The anger left him suddenly, making him feel tired and helpless. He sat on the edge of the bed, put his head in his hands, and closed his eyes.

"Hey..." He felt the bed dip as O'Brian came to him, and strong hands kneaded his shoulders, massaging the tension away. "Look, Nick, I don't know what we're gonna do, but we've only got an hour to decide. We better talk."

"What's to talk about -- who gets to be on top?" Valenti asked bitterly. "No, wait, that's already been established. *I* get the honor."

"I'd rather you do me than one of those goons," O'Brian said. "Babe, you're gonna have to face it -- we're between a rock and a hard place here."

"Poor choice of words, partner, wouldn't you say?" But Valenti sat up straighter and at least looked at his partner. O'Brian looked a lot more relaxed than Valenti could have believed possible. He sat quietly beside Valenti, still nude, but not uncomfortable in his nudity. O'Brian had always had an animal comfort in his own skin that Valenti admired immensely.

"What do you want me to say?" Valenti asked at last. "How am I supposed to feel about this? About being forced to...to force myself on you?"

"Hey, nobody's forcin' anybody," O'Brian protested, sliding closer so that Valenti could feel the body heat from his partner's naked skin like a line of fire along his side. "Conrad may be able to make us do this, but he can't make us hate each other over it. Can't really make us hurt each other."

"Oh, you don't think it's going to hurt? Having my cock rammed up your ass?" Valenti asked roughly, turning on the man beside him. Valenti shook his head and closed his eyes tightly. "Sorry, I didn't mean that," he said quickly. "It's just that...hell, Sean, I've never done anything like this before -- not even with a woman. I don't know the first thing about it. How am I gonna do it without hurting you and making you hate me?"

"Could never hate you." O'Brian swallowed thickly and looked up into Valenti's eyes. "I love you, babe. Won't blame you for doin' what ya gotta do."

"That's what this whole assignment has been about -- doing what we have to do. I wish to God we'd never accepted it in the first place," Valenti said bitterly, turning away again. "But, Sean, I don't want to do this to you. Not...not this way." It was the closest he could come to saying what was in his heart. *I don't want to do this with you out of necessity instead of love.* "Don't want to fuck you this way," he said at last, unable to meet the sea-green eyes.

"Then don't," O'Brian said quietly.

Valenti looked at him. "What do you mean? You've just been sitting here telling me how we have no choice. It's me or the goons; isn't that right?"

"Don't fuck me, I mean." O'Brian looked at him seriously and placed one hand on his partner's thigh. "Make love to me, babe. We've been everything to each other, everything but this. Now we'll just, well, take the last step."

Valenti looked at him, speechless. *But how do you know we can take that step back once we get out of here?* The way he knew O'Brian would want to.

"It doesn't have to be ugly or hateful," O'Brian continued earnestly, his hand massaging Valenti's thigh as he spoke. "It can be a beautiful thing, Valenti. An expression of our friendship. Our partnership. The ultimate." Sea-green eyes pleaded with him to understand.

The ultimate sacrifice, Valenti thought, looking down at the hand on his thigh. *The ultimate expression of friendship, but not love. And when we get out of here, the memory will rip us apart, and then we won't even have our friendship left. You'll leave me, Sean; you won't be able to help it. Because every time you look at me, it won't be your best friend and partner you see. I'll be the man you gave it up for -- the man who fucked you. And nothing I can do or say will change that. I've lost you, here and now, whether you know it or not. This is the end of the line, pal. It's all over.*

"All right," he said heavily. "How do you want to do it?" He stood and began rapidly stripping off his clothes until he was as nude as his partner. The mirrored walls reflected back his own dark skin, such a contrast to O'Brian's pale golden pelt. The images of light and dark mocked him as he stood at the foot of the bed.

"Boy, you're romantic, aren't ya?" O'Brian muttered. Lying back on the bed, he looked at Valenti and beckoned him with one hand. "C'mere," he said at last. Hesitating only briefly, Valenti did. He lay stiffly by his partner's side until O'Brian curled himself around the longer body and nuzzled into his neck.

"What are you doing?" Valenti asked, his voice breaking just a little as O'Brian's hand played over his chest, pinching his nipples into awareness.

"Lovin' you, babe. Wish you'd love me back," came the breathless whisper, and a hot tongue flicked briefly against the side of his throat, making Valenti catch his breath with tension and need. O'Brian leaned over him then, supporting his weight on one elbow, and came in for a kiss. As his partner's soft red lips met his and he felt O'Brian's hot tongue invading his mouth, Valenti knew he was lost. With a groan, he tangled his fingers in the thicket of red-gold hair and pulled O'Brian closer.

"Oh, God, Sean. Wish it didn't have to be this way," he whispered when they parted at last, both panting from emotion.

"It is what it is," his partner answered enigmatically. "Can't help it now, babe, just gotta go with the flow. So make love with me -- please?"

"You want to get it over with? Is that it?" Valenti asked sadly, looking into the beloved eyes fringed thickly with gold.

"No...well, I admit it's a little scary." O'Brian's voice dropped a little, and he caressed Valenti's cheek gently with one finger as he spoke. "But I can't quite explain. It's almost like...I've been waitin' for this ever since we got here. Like it was fate, indelible, ya know?"

"Inevitable," Valenti corrected automatically with a small, sad smile. "I know. I felt it, too." And he had. He vividly remembered the deep feeling of unease he'd had ever since they accepted the case. "I knew this would change us forever the first day we got here. Don't know how, I just knew," he said, verbalizing the feeling to his partner.

"Nothin' has to change," O'Brian insisted. "It'll still be you and me -- us against them forever, partner. You know that."

"O'Brian, how can you lie there, getting ready to let me fuck you, and say nothing's going to change?" Valenti demanded. He rolled them over suddenly so that the weight of his body was pressing the smaller man into the plush mattress, holding his partner's arms above his head.

He looked down at O'Brian, searching the sea-green depths for signs of unease, but all he saw was a calm determination. *Gonna take it like a man, aren't you?* he thought, filled with unwilling admiration. He wondered if he could have been so sanguine about the situation if their positions were reversed and doubted it. Still, he couldn't let it go.

"You like this?" Valenti ground his pelvis against O'Brian's, feeling his aching cock grow hard at the touch of his partner's shaft, which was already a bar of hot steel branding his lower belly. "You think this won't change us?" He was going to lose his best friend forever, and a perverse part of him wanted to rub it in -- to makes sure O'Brian knew that Valenti knew exactly what was going on. That he understood just how much he was losing.

"You think when you look at me when we get out of this place that it'll be in the same way -- with the same eyes? Hell no!" He gave a sharp thrust against his partner's belly, grinding their cocks together with a vicious friction that forced a hiss from between O'Brian's teeth. "When we get out of here and you look at me, you won't see your best friend, your partner. You're going to see the man that *fucked* you, Sean. And you're going to *hate* me for it." His own eyes searched sea green with blazing intensity, daring his partner to contradict him. "You know it's true -- admit it," Valenti demanded harshly.

"Admit what -- that I'll hate you when this is over?" With a sudden move, O'Brian was on top, straddling Valenti's thighs and staring down at him with something like anger. "When are you gonna get it through that thick skull of yours that nothin' you could do to me would make me hate you? Why are you doing this, Nick? You want me to make it easy on you? You want me to beg for it?" O'Brian rubbed himself roughly along the length of Valenti's body, like a cat in heat. Leaning down, he tongued and nipped Valenti's nipples, sucking until his partner gasped and arched up to get more of the agonizing pleasure.

"No, I...oh, God, Sean..." Valenti groaned as O'Brian held him down and kissed him, licking long, wet furrows across his chest and flanks with a single-minded intensity.

"Fine." O'Brian looked up at last, panting, cheeks flushed and eyes bright as he surveyed Valenti, held captive beneath him. "Fine, I *want* you to fuck me. Is that what you need to hear to make this right? To make it easy on you? I wanna feel you inside me -- inside my body -- fillin' me up with your thick cock. So fuck me, Nick. Do it now, 'cause I can't wait anymore. Do it *now.*"

O'Brian rolled off him suddenly and turned onto his stomach, his face in the pillow, legs spread and ass in the air. *Presenting*, Valenti thought, sick with shame and desire. *Opening himself for me. Offering his body for me to take -- to plunder -- to fuck.* His cock was harder than it ever had been in his life, and he hated himself for it. How could he want to do this to his partner -- the man he loved most in the world? How could he long for this loss of innocence, this violation of his partner's body and everything they held between them as sacred? And yet he did. God help him, he did.

Valenti longed to plunge hilt-deep into the willing flesh of his partner's body. His cock ached to be encased in that warm haven. He wanted to punish O'Brian for putting these thoughts -- these unnatural urges -- into his head in the first place. For being so beautiful and so willing to touch and be touched. For tempting him to this sin -- this shame -- this ultimate betrayal. *But I'll get him ready first. I'll be damned if I'll rape him cold, or I'm no better than one of Conrad's goons.*

Roughly he grabbed O'Brian's arm and turned the other man over. "Wha--?" O'Brian began, but Valenti didn't give him time to finish the thought. With one motion, he had the other man flat on his back and O'Brian's weeping cock buried deep in his throat. He had never done this before, had never even dreamed of it until the last month, when his attraction for his partner finally made itself known, but it seemed he knew instinctively what to do.

"Oh, God...Nick!" came the low groan from O'Brian's throat, but Valenti paid no attention to that; he was too involved in his work, in completing the task he had set himself. He would suck O'Brian dry, he decided. He would at least give his partner that much pleasure before he did the unthinkable...the inevitable. *Rape.*

"God, babe...oh!" Warm fingers tangled in his hair as Valenti took the wide cock down his throat, sucking like his life depended on it, giving a fierce pleasure that O'Brian accepted with difficulty. The shaft in his mouth was satiny-smooth, faintly musky, and utterly delicious. O'Brian was thicker than him, Valenti noted almost clinically as he sucked. Thicker, but not quite as long. He fondled the tight sac at the base of the cock, felt it drawing up as his partner's body prepared to come.

"Valenti, no...gonna come. Gonna..." Valenti paid not the slightest attention to the hoarse protests or O'Brian's feeble attempts to yank him up by the hair. *Gonna taste you, babe*, he thought with grim determination. *Gonna swallow your load, every drop. It's the least I can do.*

"God…Ohgodohgodohgod…" O'Brian was moaning and bucking beneath him now. Dimly Valenti was aware that the fingers that had been trying to pull him away were now holding his head in place as O'Brian fucked deeply into his mouth.

Valenti tightened his grip on the base of his partner's shaft and increased his suction, breathing through his nose and ignoring his aching jaw. He wanted to taste O'Brian's cum, wanted to feel that bitter, salty heat spurt across his tongue before he buried himself to the hilt in his partner's body and destroyed their friendship forever.

At last it happened. With a final, desperate groan, O'Brian pushed deep into his mouth, and Valenti felt the solid muscles of O'Brian's thighs turn to iron as the salty jets hit the back of his throat like a bitter benediction. Moaning, nearly sobbing with release, O'Brian caressed his scalp, his fingers carding through Valenti's hair, fiercely gentle with the intensity of his emotion.

Valenti felt the cock in his mouth begin to lose its aching thickness and pulled slowly away. He looked up to see sea green swallowed by the black of O'Brian's pupils looking back. There was an expression, a tenderness in his partner's eyes that he couldn't bear to see. Not now. Now when he was preparing to do this thing that would bring an end to their friendship for all time.

"Was it good?" he asked, sorry that the words came out so harshly, but unable to help his tone.

"God, babe." O'Brian swallowed thickly and reached down to caress a strand of raven hair out of Valenti's eyes. Valenti jerked away. "Better than good," O'Brian said gently. "Nobody's ever loved me like that before, Valenti. Nobody."

"Hope you're ready for more loving, then." Valenti hated the harsh, demanding tone in his voice, but didn't know how to stop it. He stared fiercely down at his partner until the other man dropped his gaze, the goldish-red lashes like fans across the high, tanned cheekbones.

"How do you need me, babe?" O'Brian whispered. Valenti found himself unable to answer, but O'Brian acted anyway, rolling once more onto his stomach and spreading his legs for his partner's assault.

Valenti found he was obscurely glad that his partner had picked this position for their coupling. *At least now I won't have to look in your eyes while I hurt you*, he thought sadly. But he wouldn't hurt his partner any more than he could help it.

Remembering what Conrad had said, he fumbled in the drawer of the nightstand closest to him and found a small container of lube. Hands shaking, he managed to open it and squeeze a small amount onto his fingers. Trembling, he spread the firm cheeks before him and pressed one wet finger inside O'Brian's body.

A deep, jagged breath was the only indication that his partner felt the invasion. "You okay?" Valenti asked roughly, trying to go slow as he pressed into the burning heat he desperately craved.

"Yeah." O'Brian didn't seem willing to say much, only spread his legs a little wider and buried his face in the pillow. "Go on, babe. Do it." The voice was muffled but determined. Valenti had a sudden memory of Twonnie saying, "It takes a lot more guts to take it than to dish it out."

He felt a rush of respect for his partner, lying so quietly while Valenti prepared to take him -- to use him in a way no man should have to endure from his worst enemy, let alone his best friend. The agony flared in his heart as he carefully inserted another finger and stretched, feeling the tight ring of muscle give slowly as O'Brian tried to relax and accept his invading fingers. But his cock was as hard and needful as ever, with a mindless lust that didn't care about anything but animal gratification.

Valenti hated himself, because he knew that even without Conrad's threat hanging over them, he still would have wanted to do this. Still would've wanted to plunder his partner's body like so much mindless, willing flesh.

"Do it now." O'Brian's words broke his concentration, and Valenti realized that the pale golden body beneath him was trembling with a mixture of fear and anticipation. O'Brian had bunched a pillow under his abdomen in order to raise his ass to the right height for fucking, and he was spread, naked and waiting for his partner to do what had to be done. "Do it," O'Brian whispered brokenly, his face still turned so that Valenti couldn't see his eyes. "Do it, Valenti. Can't wait any longer. Need to have you in me. Need to feel you *fuck* me."

The words drove him over the edge. Valenti spread more of the gel onto his shaft and fit himself against his partner's body without further hesitation, pressing the thick head of his cock to the tight entrance O'Brian presented. "God," he whispered, pressing inward and feeling the muscles under his hands jump and bunch with tension as his partner struggled to accept Valenti's thickness into his body. "Sorry, I'm so sorry..." he whispered as he pressed inward, invading the loving flesh, filling his partner with himself, with his cock.

"Don't...don't be," O'Brian gasped, trying to hold still as Valenti sank his cock deeper and deeper. "Just do it, babe. Just fuck me. Know you need it...I need it, too. Need to feel you in me."

He raised his head at last, and Valenti could see tears of pain in the deep-green eyes reflected in the mirrored wall behind the bed. Pain, but no blame. He reached up and felt an answering salty wetness on his own cheeks, and still his cock was hard with wanting, with needing. *I'm an animal -- no matter how much it hurts him I can't stop.* The thought was a knife in his heart.

The images in the mirror seemed to mock him. Before him, a dark man crouched above a golden one, impaling him as two sets of eyes watched, one set gone from brown to black in anguish, the other like the sea after a storm. Dark eclipsing light. Valenti thought the scene in the mirror looked like a demon raping an angel.

At last he felt himself enveloped down to the root and heard O'Brian gasp, "In me so deep, babe. God, so *deep!*" Valenti waited for a moment, grasping his partner's hips in his hands, trying to still the hammering of his heart. Then, closing his eyes, hating himself more than he had ever thought possible, he began to thrust.

The friction around his shaft was indescribable -- wet velvet that gripped and clung to his every contour as he moved inside O'Brian's body. Valenti pulled back, feeling the slick fist of his partner's inner muscles around his shaft, and pushed forward again, plundering, taking what his body begged for.

He felt a need for even deeper penetration, and leaning back for greater leverage, he thrust again, harder this time. It seemed that the new position did something to O'Brian, touched a spot inside his body that galvanized his partner like an electric shock. Valenti felt him jump as he plowed forward, and thought, *Prostate.* A low groan from the man under him confirmed the thought.

"God, Nick...what?" O'Brian moaned, hands gripping the coverlet beneath them as he struggled to be open enough for Valenti's cock, struggled to take the punishing pleasure Valenti was ramming into his body with each thrust of his thick shaft.

Without answering, Valenti took full advantage of the situation. *At least I can give you some pleasure while I'm doing this to you.* Keeping the angle so that he ground himself mercilessly over and over that one spot in his partner's body, he began to fuck in earnest, pounding into O'Brian's body, letting go as he had never dared to do with any woman he had ever been with. Somewhere inside him, a voice whispered that his partner could take it. O'Brian was no soft, easily damaged female who might cry out and beg Valenti to stop. He was strong enough to take all the rough love his partner had to offer and ask for more. O'Brian's next words confirmed his thoughts.

"Ah, Nicky... Nick! You're fuckin' me so good, babe. So deep. Don't stop...harder!"

"Is this what you want? Is it?" Valenti demanded, driven crazy by the intense sensations around his cock and his partner's provocative words. He thrust harder, deeper, clutching O'Brian's hips so fiercely that he knew there would be finger-shaped bruises bracketing his partner's pelvis the next day. And yet he didn't care -- didn't care about anything but owning this man who was gasping and begging beneath him. Possessing his partner utterly, marking him, *branding* him so that neither of them could ever forget Valenti's cock buried to the hilt in O'Brian's unresisting flesh.

"Like that -- just like *that!*" O'Brian gasped, and Valenti watched in the mirrored wall as his partner orgasmed again. *Coming so hard,* he thought distractedly as the sea-green eyes squeezed shut with the intense mixture of pain and pleasure. O'Brian's body gripped his cock in a spasm of pure emotion.

And then Valenti was coming, too, was ramming himself hilt-deep in his partner, as though trying to reach the other man's heart with his cock, as he cried out his wordless pain and shame and pleasure at the release he found in O'Brian's body.

Never had sex been this intense, this agonizingly pleasurable. And never had Valenti hated himself more. Gasping, he pulled out abruptly, feeling O'Brian's body contract around him and hearing the other man's hiss of pain at the too-quick departure. Feeling ragged, emotionally and physically spent, he turned away from the pale golden flesh and slid wearily under the covers.

He knew he ought to stay awake and alert for Conrad and his goons, but he couldn't make himself care. *That's it, Nicholas*, he thought tiredly. *Hope you enjoyed it. Hope what you just did was pleasurable enough to justify ending the most important relationship in your life.* Burying his head under a pillow, he let exhaustion take him. Just before he drifted off, he thought he felt a gentle hand on the back of his neck.

"'S Okay, babe," whispered a voice. "You rest now, take it easy."

"Sean," he tried to say. "I'm so sorry...so Goddamn sorry." But his vocal chords were already paralyzed by sleep, and then the blackness took him.

Chapter Fifteen

A hand shaking him woke him up, but not completely. "Jus' a minute, Sean," he muttered, not wanting to leave the warm confines of the bed. "Almos' awake. Harris doesn't expect us in till nine anyway…"

"Wake up, Valenti." The voice wasn't his partner's, but rather that of the man he had been speaking of. Valenti's eyes flew open, blinded at first by the light but adjusting quickly to see his captain standing at the side of the bed.

"Where's O'Brian?" he asked at once, and then remembering what had happened between them, he said quickly, "Never mind." Harris, who was leaning over the bed, gave him a questioning look, but answered the question anyway.

"Your partner is already on his way back to the Metro to give a statement. He said to tell you he'll see you later on. You could have gone with him, but you wouldn't wake up. I've been shaking you for the last ten minutes. Was beginning to think I'd have to find some cold water to pour on your face." He shook his head, frowning disapprovingly.

"But…" Valenti sat up in bed, aware that he was still stark naked and glad for the coverlet bunched in his lap. "What about Conrad? What about the guards?"

"Taken care of," Harris said dismissively. "We found out just this morning there was a mole in the Frisco PD -- one of Conrad's men -- and we knew your cover was blown. Sure am glad we got to you before anything happened."

Oh, Captain, you have no idea how much has happened. You're late -- much, much too late. Valenti only shook his head. Then he remembered something else. "There was a film... Conrad said..." He couldn't finish, but he didn't have to.

Harris gave him a penetrating look and answered, "That was O'Brian's first concern, as well. We found a room with some equipment, and I allowed him to take what he wanted with the understanding that he would view it and let me know if any of it should be considered evidence."

Valenti sagged in relief at his captain's words. O'Brian would be able to destroy the evidence of their shame. No matter how badly it might affect their partnership, the film at least wouldn't end their careers. Then he wondered how much his career was worth to him now that his friendship with O'Brian was surely over anyway.

"Get dressed; we're leaving in five." Harris threw him a bundle of clothes and walked out of the room, leaving Valenti with his thoughts.

* * *

"Valenti, my office, *now.*" Captain Harris's voice was angry, and Valenti winced as he rose from his desk, avoiding his partner's worried eyes, and walked into the office. "What is the meaning of this?" Harris barked. Valenti barely had a chance to close the door and sit down. Harris was waving a white piece of paper that Valenti recognized immediately.

"Request for transfer, Captain," he said quietly.

"You want to tell me why, Detective Valenti?" Harris demanded, his voice gone dangerously soft and low.

"Not really," Valenti answered coolly. Then, before Harris could explode, he asked, "How much has O'Brian told you about our last day at the RamJack?"

Harris blushed suddenly, his cheeks going a dull brick red. "He...uh, did say some things were done -- unavoidable things. Completely unavoidable, given the nature of your assignment. Detective Valenti." The captain looked up, embarrassment suddenly forgotten, and stared Valenti straight in the eye. "Detective O'Brian told me that you both did what you had to do. I can assure you that none of it is getting anywhere near your permanent record."

"It's not the permanent record I'm worried about, Captain," Valenti said quietly. "If O'Brian told you anything at all, then you should know that I ought to be buried *under* the jail for what I did to him. I... Captain, I can't stay here anymore, not with O'Brian for a partner. And if O'Brian was honest, he'd probably tell you he doesn't want me for a partner, either. He doesn't need me around here reminding him of what happened between us."

"That's not the impression I got at all. Why don't you go home and sleep on this, Valenti? It's only been a week since you and O'Brian came back from Frisco," Harris pointed out. "I know this last assignment strained your relationship with your partner, but give it some time."

"All the time in the world won't help," Valenti said in a low voice. "Some things, when you break them, can't ever be put back together again. This is one of those things, Captain."

"Valenti, I can't believe this is really what's best for you and your partner. You and Detective O'Brian are two of my finest. I refuse to lose you over a stupid misunderstanding. Now, go home and get some rest. That's an order," Harris said sternly. "It's clear to me that I asked you to come back to active duty before you were ready. Sleep on this --" He waved the transfer form. "-- and talk to me again on Monday. All right? Dismissed."

Valenti got up and left silently. He gathered his things from his desk and, ignoring O'Brian's worried questions, headed for home.

Chapter Sixteen

"Valenti, open the door. Damn it, I know you're in there. Open up!" The loud pounding on his door resumed, and Valenti reluctantly acknowledged to himself that O'Brian wasn't likely to give up anytime soon. He had moved the key from its usual position over the door specifically so his partner would take the hint and leave him alone, but O'Brian had never been one to take a hint if he didn't want to.

"What do you want?" he asked through the closed door. He had been avoiding a scene just like this all week, trying to keep a safe distance between himself and his partner, and O'Brian had seemed willing to let him -- had seemed willing to give him space. Valenti had been hoping that the uneasy truce between them would last until his transfer came through, but apparently that wasn't going to happen. "What do you want?" he asked again, one hand on the knob.

"What do you think I want, Valenti? To talk, damn it! We gotta stop tip-toin' around each other and talk this out."

"There's nothing to talk about." Valenti opened the door a crack to look out at his partner, and that was all the encouragement O'Brian needed. He pushed his way into the house and slammed the door behind him. With one hand on Valenti's shoulder, he propelled the taller man to the couch and pressed firmly until Valenti dropped unresisting onto the cushions.

"There's a hell of a lot to talk about, and you know it," O'Brian snapped, standing over him, scowling.

"Maybe I just need some time," Valenti offered weakly, not meeting O'Brian's eyes, which had turned a hard, sharp emerald with frustration.

"I've tried to give you time, Valenti. Tried to leave you alone while you thought it through -- what happened between us, I mean -- and look where it got us. You askin' Harris for a transfer. Why would you go and do that?"

"You know damn well why!" Valenti snapped back impatiently. "And what the hell business of yours is it, anyway?"

The expression on O'Brian's face was both frustrated and tender as he sat beside Valenti and looked at his partner for a long moment before replying. "It's my business the same way everything that affects you is my business. Because we're partners. Because we're friends. Come on, Nick, you know that. Don't be like this with me."

"I don't know any other way to be since...what happened. What I did to you." Valenti looked up briefly and then down again at his hands.

"What we did to each other, you mean." O'Brian took one of Valenti's hands, dangling limply between Valenti's legs, and entwined their fingers. "You didn't hurt me, didn't force me to do anything I didn't want to do."

"How can you say that?" Valenti exploded, angrily pulling his hand away. "I *fucked* you. And goddammit..." His voice dropped as the anger suddenly fell away, leaving only pain and shame behind. "I enjoyed it." Valenti looked up, searching the sea-green eyes for a moment before dropping his own.

"I enjoyed it, too," O'Brian said quietly. "Is that really such a problem?"

"You don't understand. You couldn't." It felt like ripping his heart out to say the words, but Valenti couldn't stop them coming. "It was like even if I hurt you, I couldn't stop. Couldn't...couldn't get enough of you. I wanted you so *bad*. It was like a sickness in me -- like a hunger I couldn't control. I hate myself for doing that to you."

"I don't hate you, babe," was the quiet response. O'Brian took his hand again, and this time Valenti let him hold it, taking comfort in the warm, solid grip of his partner's fingers against his own. "Why should you hate yourself? Why can't you just accept that we did what we had to do and move on?"

"Because." Valenti looked up, meeting his partner's eyes, letting O'Brian see the naked truth in his own. "The whole time we were there, I wasn't just doing what I had to do undercover. I was doing what I *wanted* to do. I *wanted* to touch you and kiss you, and hell, Sean, I wanted to *fuck* you. Wanted it so bad I couldn't see straight. I'm in love with you, goddammit, and I can't go back to the way we were before this assignment." He took a trembling breath.

"Now do you see why I have to go? I can't keep on with this stupid act we have between us. Can't keep on pretending that we're best friends, partners, whatever the hell you want to call us, when all I want to do..." He sighed heavily. "...is hold you tight and never let go."

O'Brian's face was a complete blank. Valenti felt like a man who had gambled everything and lost. He stood up, pulling his hand away from his partner's, and turned his back. "You can leave anytime," he said stiffly, crossing his arms over his chest and staring at the floor. "I know you probably want to."

"What the hell do you know about what I want?" O'Brian's voice was ragged.

Valenti felt a hand on his shoulder before he was dragged around and O'Brian's mouth was branding his own. For a moment he was too stunned to react, and then he opened his lips to allow better access, and the sweet taste of his partner, his best friend, his *lover* was flooding his senses like a drug.

O'Brian dug frantic fingers into his hair and pulled him close, ravishing his mouth, claiming him, marking Valenti as his exclusive territory. *Guess I'm not the only one who feels possessive*, Valenti thought. But then the kiss deepened, and all conscious thought was driven out of his head by pleasure and need.

They fell apart at last, gasping, and the look in O'Brian's sea-green eyes was utterly wild. Valenti put a hand to his bottom lip, feeling a warm, wet trickle, and pulled it back to see a small smear of blood on his finger. "You bit me," he said, eyes wide.

"Damn right." O'Brian pulled him in again and sucked at the small wound, licking aggressively before releasing him reluctantly. "How long?" O'Brian asked, frowning.

Valenti understood. "Since about a month before the RamJack. It just kind of, I don't know, *hit* me all at once, but I think it had been building up for a long time. Years, maybe. And when I almost lost you after the stabbing... I think I finally realized how I really felt. How much I needed you. After a while it got to be all I could think about; it was driving me *crazy*. How long for you?"

"While we were there," O'Brian admitted in a low voice. "Well, maybe before, but I didn't really *know* it till we got there and started playin' those parts. It was like I had the feelings, but no name to stick on 'em, ya know?"

"Yeah, I know," Valenti agreed quietly. His partner took a step forward and took both his hands, entwining their fingers again, pulling him close.

"Why the hell didn't you say anything before, Nicky?" he demanded.

"How could I?" Valenti gave his partner an aggrieved look from under furrowed brows. "When I knew how you felt about gays? After your brother Ian came out and you were so upset --"

"What upset me about Ian was the way he hurt the other people in his life. Leavin' his wife and kids like that -- he should never have gotten married in the first place. He should have just come out instead of tryin' to deny what he was. The same way we've been denyin' how we feel about each other." O'Brian shook his head angrily. "Damn it, Nick, what about that story I told about our 'first time' at dinner that first night? I threw ya every hint in the book."

"*And* you kept saying that we were just doing what we had to do while we were undercover," Valenti pointed out, dropping his partner's hands to cross his arms. He saw no reason to take all the blame for their mutual misunderstanding. O'Brian could be so damned *annoying* at times.

"Well, I was gettin' plenty of mixed signals from you, too, pal." O'Brian looked just as irritated as Valenti felt. "Why'd you keep sayin' you'd never forget our time together, like everything had to be over when we finished the bust?"

"I didn't want to crowd you. I thought you *wanted* me to let you off the hook -- like it was a one-time-only deal," Valenti explained.

"Why'd you keep sayin' it was gonna *change* us? Like it was the worst thing in the world, or somethin'?" O'Brian was obviously still upset.

"Well, it did, didn't it? Look at us." Valenti gestured between them with one hand. "We didn't used to act this way, kissing each other, holding hands..." His voice trailed off, and he could feel a blush creeping up his cheeks.

"You sayin' you don't like it?" O'Brian asked quietly. "Us feelin' this way about each other, I mean?"

"Yes...no...I don't know." Valenti collapsed wearily onto the couch and put his head in his hands. "I don't like the way it made me treat you, Sean," he said at last. "The way it made me act toward you. What I did to you...'Brian threw up his hands in disgust. "Not *this* again. Look, Nicky, how many times do I have to tell you? I liked it, too! I wanted it -- wanted *you*. So what if you got a little rough at the end? I'd been drivin' you nuts by every possible means for the past two days and nights. I tell you what." His voice dropped, and he leaned down to get a good look in Valenti's anguished eyes. "If Conrad hadn't put us in that damn glass box, I was gonna try and get you to do it that night anyway."

"Really?" Valenti felt a little shocked. He had seen O'Brian when he was in pursuit of a woman he liked and knew how single-minded his partner could be, but he had never expected to have that possessive determination turned on himself. "You mean..." He cleared his throat and sat up a little. "You mean, you were going to try to get me to...to do you?"

"To fuck me, yes," O'Brian said shortly. "Don't get me wrong, babe, I was willing to go the other way, too, but you seemed like you'd be more open to bein' the one on top, so to speak." He shrugged. "Didn't really matter to me so long as we ended up together in the end. So..." He looked anxiously at his partner. "How do you...you know, feel about all this?"

"Give me a minute. Just..." Valenti shook his head. He didn't know quite *how* to feel. Angry that O'Brian had been manipulating him. Flattered that his partner wanted him so much. Disgusted at himself for selling them both short... The list just went on and on. O'Brian was giving him time to think, but it was obviously hard on the man, who was sitting on the couch beside him, fidgeting like a kid who had to pee. Finally, O'Brian burst out, "Well?"

Valenti looked at his partner's anxious, beautiful face and wanted to smile. Wanted to, but didn't quite. "I don't know, partner," he said at last. "I can't tell you how I feel because I still don't know where we stand. What does this make us? Do we try to go back to being just friends? Because I don't think I can do that."

"No, we're a lot more than that now." O'Brian's expression softened. "I think we've been more than just friends for a long time, only we didn't know it."

"Yeah." Valenti allowed himself a tiny smile. "You're right about that, but that still doesn't give me any idea what we're doing here, Sean. Are we lovers? Or just fuck buddies? Are we exclusive?" He shook his head. "See what I mean? It's pretty complicated."

"No, it's not," O'Brian countered fiercely, leaning forward to make his point. "You belong to me, and I belong to you. What could be simpler than that? Nick, if I can have you, I don't want or need anything or anybody else in the world. Call it whatever you want. Just say *yes*."

He looked so nervous and sincere that Valenti grinned at him openly. "Sounds like you're asking me to marry you or something," he said. "Where's the ring?"

"I'm not joking around here, Nicky," O'Brian said earnestly. "Look, what we've got between us, well, it's a lot better than any marriage *I* ever heard of. What we've been though together, the way we've been there for each other... We have a true partnership, a true *love*, and if that sounds stupid and romantic, then I don't care." He leaned forward and kissed Valenti on the lips, gently at first, as if he wasn't quite sure of his reception.

Valenti sighed and leaned into the kiss, parting his lips to welcome his partner's tongue, feeling like he was melting from the waist down. What was it about this man whom he had known for so long and so well that could move him so much? Blood throbbed in his cock, making him feel that burning need, the urge to possess O'Brian completely. To be possessed by him, as well, Valenti realized.

When they pulled apart, they were both panting a little, and O'Brian gave him that irrepressible grin. "What about that, huh?" he asked, still cupping Valenti's cheek in one hand. "When I kiss you, touch you...it's like I'm on fire, babe. I want you so *bad*. Haven't felt this horny since I was in high school."

"There *is* that," Valenti admitted, turning his head to nuzzle the beloved hand. God, but it felt good to have O'Brian's hands on him again. *Missed you so much, babe*. He cleared his throat and forced himself to move back some and get a little distance. "Sean, I have to say I feel the same way about you that you feel about me --"

"I love you, Nick," O'Brian broke in, his whole heart in the words and in the honest, open face Valenti loved so much. "More than anything, more than anybody. You're the only one for me, *ever*." O'Brian closed his eyes and took a deep breath as though this little speech had been bursting to get out of him and now, having said it, he could relax.

"Ah, Sean... Valenti couldn't talk for a moment, overcome by the emotion of his partner's declaration. He felt like his heart might swell right out of his chest. Impulsively, he leaned forward, cupped his partner's face, and kissed both O'Brian's eyelids gently, tasting salty moisture on his lips as he pulled back. "Back at you, partner," he managed to say at last. "I love you, too. I just want to know where we're headed with this."

"Right now I want to be headed to bed." The intensity was like green fire in O'Brian's eyes, the raw hunger evident in his expression. "You haven't let me touch you in nearly a week, babe. I'm burnin' up, I want you so bad."

"Want you, too, Sean," Valenti whispered. "Only..."

"What? Name it. Anything you want." O'Brian was looking at him the way a starving wolf might look at a steak. Valenti didn't know whether to laugh or give in to the incredible desire flowing between them like an electric current. He took his partner's hand

and felt the jolt of it hit him in the belly, the need like a sucker-punch that took away all his breath. Suddenly the situation wasn't the least bit funny.

"I just…I felt so bad last time we…did what we did." Valenti murmured. "I felt like I was hurting you…forcing you. I know." He held up a hand to forestall O'Brian's protests. "I know better now. But still, I just…I don't know if I want to do it that way for a while. You know?"

"I understand, babe. We don't have to do anything until you want to, I swear." O'Brian's sweet words belied the growing bulge in the tight jeans he wore. Valenti hastened to reassure him.

"No, I want to…be with you. Just…not *that* way, okay?" He didn't know why he felt so shy and awkward about expressing what he wanted to his partner. Some things, he reflected, are harder to talk about than to do.

"Then how?" O'Brian looked puzzled, and Valenti realized they would need a bit more clarification to make things work.

"The other way. I mean, with you… Valenti cleared his throat. This was getting them nowhere. "O'Brian," he said directly, even though he felt his face turning beet red. "What I'm trying to say is, I want you to…to fuck me."

The look on his partner's face was downright feral. "Thought you'd never ask," he growled, pulling Valenti in for another long, hungry kiss. "My pleasure, babe."

Chapter Seventeen

Valenti didn't know how they got to the bed, but suddenly they were there, rolling around on the bedspread, coming up for air only long enough for O'Brian to say, "In your bed. Just like my story, huh, babe?" Remembering his partner's bogus "first time" story that night at the RamJack made Valenti hot all over again. He felt like he couldn't get himself and his partner undressed fast enough. His pants were barely off when O'Brian pushed him over onto his back and swallowed his cock hungrily, hands splayed across Valenti's chest and abdomen to hold him in place.

"Ah, God...Sean!" Valenti gasped, hips pumping rhythmically into that warm, wet enclosure. "So good..."

"Gonna make you come, babe." O'Brian looked up briefly, and Valenti could feel his partner's hot breath on his cock as he spoke. "Gonna make you come, and then I'm gonna fuck you so *deep*. Can't wait to be inside you." And then he went back to work on Valenti, sucking and licking and squeezing until Valenti thought he would faint or explode. He felt the sensations building to a peak rapidly and tangled his fingers in the soft, reddish-gold hair to urge O'Brian closer.

Understanding, as he always did, exactly what Valenti needed, O'Brian ducked lower, and then Valenti felt the indescribable sensation of his cock being literally swallowed as O'Brian took him all the way down, the pale, beautiful throat working convulsively.

"Sean! God! Love you so much!" Valenti gasped, feeling as though the cum was being *pulled* out of him. His back arched helplessly, and he seemed to come endlessly, spasming over and over as O'Brian sucked and milked him for every last drop before finally releasing him. "God, Sean…that was fucking *amazing*," he panted at last while his partner grinned, the golden head still resting on Valenti's belly.

"Love the way you taste, babe. Love to go down on you."

"You're damn good at it," Valenti said, still breathing heavily. "Give any pro I ever met a run for her money."

"Gee, thanks," O'Brian said dryly. "Think I oughta consider a career change?"

"Not a chance," Valenti told him, ruffling the blond thatch affectionately. "The only cock I ever better catch you sucking is mine, partner."

"Same goes for you." O'Brian crawled to the head of the bed and kissed him deeply, feeding Valenti the taste of himself on that sweet tongue. "You're mine, babe, and I don't intend to share with anyone," O'Brian said, pulling back at last.

"Why don't you prove it?" Valenti asked, feeling his heart trip-hammer in his chest even as he spoke the words. "Or was all that big talk while you were blowing me just talk?"

"I don't make promises I can't keep, Nicky," O'Brian growled, nuzzling Valenti's throat and biting gently along the big vein pumping just under the skin. "You oughtta know that."

"Then put your money where your mouth is and fuck me, babe." Valenti's voice was low, taunting. He had always known exactly what buttons to press with O'Brian, and this was no exception. It seemed like his partner's hands were everywhere at once, touching, fondling, caressing, getting him ready to be fucked.

Somewhere, O'Brian had gotten a tube of some kind of lubricant, and it wasn't long before Valenti felt himself turned gently on his side while the other man stretched him with tender but urgent fingers. The sensation was wholly alien, but not unpleasant. It felt good to be able to relax and be this intimate, this completely open with O'Brian.

His partner was so gentle, so infinitely careful to be sure he was ready, that at last Valenti said, "Can't wait anymore, Sean. When you gonna put it in?" There was a sudden gust of hot breath in his ear, as though O'Brian had been waiting for him to say something before he dared to continue.

"You sure?" O'Brian asked at last. His fingers probed deeper as he talked, and suddenly they were rubbing something inside that nearly made Valenti jump out of his skin with a bolt of exquisite pleasure. *Like somebody stuck a firecracker inside me.*

"Feels good?" O'Brian sounded amused as he rubbed over the spot again.

"God, yes!" Valenti gasped, bucking against the man behind him. "Do it, Sean. Don't make me beg, dammit!"

"You want it that bad, huh?" The voice in his ear was low and hungry. Valenti leaned his head back to feel the warm, solid strength of O'Brian's shoulder behind him.

"You know I do." He knew it might hurt a little, maybe even a lot, but suddenly he could barely wait to feel his partner inside him. He wanted the experience -- the closeness as much or more than the pleasure. Wanted to feel like he belonged to O'Brian completely.

O'Brian's wiry chest hair brushed closely against Valenti's sweating back, and then Valenti felt the smooth, blunt head of his partner's heavy cock pressing insistently against him. There was pain now and a great deal of pressure, but Valenti closed his eyes and breathed through it, accepting the hurt as part of the deal. It would be worth it in the long run to feel the man he loved most in the world penetrating him, buried deep in his body.

O'Brian seemed to know what he was doing, moving slowly but steadily forward, hands rubbing ceaselessly over Valenti's hips in tight little circles, as though his partner wanted to pet away the brief pain he was causing. At last Valenti felt the trim waist and muscular hips flush with his body and knew O'Brian had to be all the way in.

"You okay?" O'Brian's voice in his ear was low and concerned. Valenti could feel the urgency coiled like a wire inside his partner and understood it himself -- the instinctive urge to thrust, the unbearable need to possess. He also knew O'Brian wouldn't move a muscle until Valenti told him he was ready.

"Fine," he whispered, feeling stretched to the limit with the thick cock buried inside him. "Feels...full, but not bad. Just go slow at first, okay?"

"Slow as you want, babe. *God*, you feel good around me." O'Brian's voice was strained but certain, and the movements he began to make inside Valenti were as gentle as they could be under the circumstances. *The circumstances being that my partner and best friend in the world is currently fucking me.* But the thought held no terror or disgust, only pleasure and satisfaction that he could give this to O'Brian, this ultimate gift of himself and his body. *Aw, Sean, I'm yours, body and soul. You own me.*

The movement behind him, inside him, began to increase, and then O'Brian was hitting that spot again, causing the electric waves of pleasure to crest inside him like lightning striking over the water. Valenti could feel his heart pounding like a jackhammer, and he gasped for breath as the feeling of his partner spreading him, filling him, *fucking* him went on and on. Incredibly, he could feel his cock hardening once more, even though he had come so hard when O'Brian sucked him.

"Love to love you this way, babe. Love to *fuck* you. Wanna fuck you all night." O'Brian's hot, breathless words in his ear made a counterpoint to a deep, urgent sound Valenti finally realized he was making himself. He could find no words to express the amazing, almost painful pleasure, but at the same time he couldn't be quiet -- didn't want to be quiet. He could feel himself peaking again, rising higher and higher, closer and closer to an orgasm unlike any he had ever felt before. At last he found his voice.

"Coming, Sean. Oh, God, you're making me come so hard! Fuck me! I wanna feel you fucking me so hard and deep..." Valenti heard the pleading, the need, and the submission in his voice and didn't give a damn.

This was O'Brian, his best friend, his *lover*, who was pulling these words out of him with such sweet pressure, the swift drive and thrust of his cock inside Valenti's body. Although he had never been particularly vocal during sex before, now it seemed like he couldn't shut up, didn't care if he ever shut up as long as the incredible sensation of O'Brian fucking him would go on and on and never end.

"God, babe, when you talk like that..." O'Brian panted behind him. "I'm *coming*. Coming inside you, Nicky. Oh, God, Nick...NICK!"

He felt O'Brian thrust deep and press so close to his body that for an instant it seemed like they truly were one person, and Valenti didn't know or care where his partner began and he himself ended. He felt his own body spasming endlessly around the beloved invader as O'Brian tensed against him, and then they were both sagging, gasping for breath as the moment passed slowly, dying into the brilliant white light behind his eyelids.

O'Brian was the first to speak. "You okay, babe? Was I too rough?" he asked anxiously, beginning to pull away. Valenti grasped the arm wrapped around his waist and held on.

"Not yet," he murmured. "Don't go yet." O'Brian relaxed behind him, keeping their bodies joined, but Valenti could still feel his partner's anxiety, a palpable thing in the air between them. "'M okay," he said at last. "Just worn out is all. Haven't come twice in thirty minutes since high school."

A soft chuff of laughter tickled his ear. "I know how ya feel. Felt the same way when you did me. Amazing, isn't it?"

"More than amazing. Thought the top of my head was gonna explode," Valenti explained. "Never felt anything like it. So good -- so special doing this with you, partner."

Strong arms squeezed him tightly from behind, and O'Brian's voice was suspiciously thick as he answered. "Love you so much, babe. Never wanna let you go."

"Going to have to eventually," Valenti pointed out. "Harris's used to seeing us joined at the hip, but this…"

There was a small explosion of laughter behind him that caused O'Brian to slip from his body. Valenti felt a spasm of regret, of emptiness, followed by an even stronger spasm of joy when he realized that they could repeat this act as often as they wanted to. Although the considerable tenderness he felt in his ass inclined him to think that maybe it would be a while before he was up to a repeat performance.

"Well, that took care of that problem, at least for now," O'Brian said. Valenti turned carefully to face his partner, looking into the face he knew better than his own.

"God, Sean, that was, I don't know, so special. So good with you. I never thought it could be so…" He stopped, at a loss for words. How could he explain that the act of love had never been this special, this *intimate* with anyone?

"I know. For me, too, babe," his partner answered, understanding as always.

"So what now?" Valenti asked, reaching up to caress O'Brian's face, cupping his lover's cheek in his hand. The long gold lashes fluttered down briefly, and O'Brian turned his head to leave a soft kiss on Valenti's palm.

"I was thinkin' maybe a quick shower and a nap," he answered, suppressing a yawn with obvious difficulty. "You wore me out with your tight little ass." He grinned, a lopsided slice of a smile that melted Valenti's heart all over again.

"Hey, dummy, that's not what I meant." Valenti grinned back at him affectionately.

"Yeah, I know," O'Brian said. "You wanna talk about everything and spell it all out. But I'm tellin' you, Nicky, there's no need. We belong together; we always have. And now we belong *to* each other in every sense of the word. Us against them, partner, just like always."

"Okay." Valenti yawned, feeling tired himself and willing to accept his partner's view of their new relationship. "If you say so." He snuggled closer to O'Brian, loving that he had the freedom to do so. He still felt somewhat sticky, but he thought he could live with it. Right now he just wanted that nap.

"Well, I do," O'Brian mumbled, throwing an arm over Valenti's shoulders. "So be good and go to sleep now, Nicky." Apparently he was willing to forgo the shower as well, at least for now.

"Love you." It was a whisper, almost a sigh, and Valenti wasn't really sure which one of them had said it. *Does it really matter?* He thought not. Pulling Sean O'Brian a final fraction of an inch closer and breathing in the warm scent of his partner's skin, he drifted off into oblivion, the dark head and the light resting on one pillow.

~ * ~

I'LL BE HOT FOR CHRISTMAS

Chapter One

Detective Sean O'Brian had finally had enough. It had been a solid month since he and Valenti had gotten any kind of action and he was sick of it. As he pulled his sleek '82 Chrysler Cordoba into a spot at the Spalding Convention Center downtown, O'Brian reflected that no, it had been longer than a month. Because the last time he could remember getting so much as a kind word, let alone anything else from Valenti was the night before the shooting incident.

He sighed and ran a hand through his thick, reddish blond hair as he got out of the car. "Damn shame, babe," he muttered, picturing Valenti's wounded brown eyes when Captain Harris had assigned him to "administrative leave" until the incident could be cleared through Internal Affairs. It was only supposed to take a week -- two weeks tops. But those IA bastards were taking their time and O'Brian knew that Valenti had been called in and grilled on at least three separate occasions. Even though several eye witnesses had testified that the junkie Valenti took down had been threatening him and O'Brian with a gun of his own, they still couldn't let it drop. And until they did, Valenti was a desk jockey and O'Brian was stuck with a new partner -- a rookie so wet behind the ears O'Brian had the urge to turn him around and look for the apron strings that were surely still attached.

Valenti had become irritable and depressed. He had also become hyper aware of the dangerous secret he and O'Brian shared -- the fact that ever since coming back from an undercover assignment at The RamJack, a notorious gay club in San Francisco, their partnership had grown to a whole new level. That they were lovers as well as partners -- or had been, anyway, before this whole miserable thing began.

It had been almost a year since they had admitted their feeling for each other and started an exclusive relationship -- one that was based on mutual respect as much as it was on the white-hot passion that flared between them. It had come as a complete surprise because neither partner had ever been attracted to another man before. But just because he'd never desired another man before Valenti didn't mean O'Brian found the sight of his tall, dark partner down on his knees taking O'Brian's thick cock down his throat any less exciting. God, just thinking about it was enough to give him an almost painful hard-on. Now if only he could get his stubborn partner to *do* something about it, they might be back in business, he reflected as he left the parking area and headed for the convention center.

Even before they had taken their partnership and friendship to the next level, O'Brian and Valenti had been all over each other -- always hugging and touching and generally just invading the hell out of each other's space. It was part of their partnership, part of what they were known for, and it was their easy way around each other that had landed them the RamJack assignment in the first place. But since the shooting incident and the IA investigation that had followed, Valenti flinched if O'Brian so much as touched him in public. In fact, just that afternoon O'Brian had come up behind his partner, who was sitting at his desk doing paperwork and looking tense, and tried to give him a neck rub. Valenti had flinched and pushed his hands away.

"Get off me, O'Brian," he muttered, his brown eyes scanning the crowded bullpen to see if any of the other officers had noticed the public display of affection. "We're in public here."

"Yeah, so?" O'Brian plopped himself down onto his partner's desk, sitting on the paperwork Valenti was working on and frowned.

"So? So we need to be a little more careful." Valenti's voice was low and worried. "A little more discreet. Could you get off my paperwork, please?"

"No. Look, Valenti," O'Brian said in what he thought was a reasonably low tone of voice. "We been nothin' *but* discreet for the past month. In fact, if we get any more *discreet* I'm gonna die of blue balls. Cut me a break here, huh?'

"Keep it down!" Valenti hissed, frowning at him fiercely. "You don't know who's listening."

"I know I don't give a damn." O'Brian began to get angry at that point. For the past month or longer he had been putting up with his partner's stand-offish attitude and sudden paranoia, but it was getting pretty old, in his opinion.

"Well I *do* give a damn whether we flush our careers down the toilet," Valenti answered.

"Flush our careers down the...what the hell are you talkin' about, Valenti?" O'Brian demanded. "Ya know, up until about a month ago, you and me always used to be all over each other. People talked, sure, but we didn't care. I mean, even after we came back from the RamJack and people talked even *more*, we still didn't care. But now..." He shook his head. "I don't know -- it's like you changed all of a sudden. And I don't think it's just the whole shooting thing and the IA givin' you hell, either. There's somethin' else goin' on in that thick skull of yours. So what gives?"

"I haven't changed. And all that...the way we acted, I mean...that was before." Valenti muttered, looking away and refusing to meet O'Brian's concerned green eyes.

"Before what?" O'Brian demanded. "Before this shooting thing? Or before whatever it is you're not tellin' me?"

"I don't know what you're talking about." Valenti made an effort to get back to his paperwork but O'Brian had his round, firm ass planted squarely on top of it and he wasn't budging until he'd had his say.

"Damnit, Valenti, I know things've been rough the last month or so but that's all gonna change. Things are gonna get better. And even if they don't, I'm here for you, just like always."

"Yeah, yeah…" But Valenti's prickly exterior looked like it was melting a little. His big brown eyes looked softer and the broad shoulders beneath his crisp, white cotton shirt didn't look quite so tense. It made O'Brian long to take him back to his apartment and give him a long, slow, sensual massage just as he had when they were undercover at the RamJack. Just the thought of that, of kneeling over his partner's long, lean, muscular body while they were both nude as he touched and stroked and kissed until Valenti turned over and begged to be sucked made O'Brian's heavy cock shift inside the skin-tight pants he was wearing. He seized the opportunity to lean down and whisper into his partner's ear.

"'S gonna be all right, Nick. I just want you to know I feel the same way I always have. I still want you. Still *need* you. And that's not gonna stop any time soon." O'Brian used his partner's first name on purpose, knowing that it got to Valenti like nothing else could. Sure enough, when Valenti finally looked up and met his eyes, it looked like O'Brian's tall, dark partner was really beginning to thaw.

"Sean," he murmured, daring to place one hand on O'Brian's knee. Just that one simple touch when they hadn't been together in so long made O'Brian go from half-mast to hard as a rock in a split second.

"Yeah, babe?" he said in a low, intimate voice.

"It's not that I don't feel the same way," Valenti said. "I just thought --"

"Hey, guys, what's goin' on?" The voice of Billy Hicks, O'Brian's temporary partner cut into their conversation and Valenti pulled his hand away from O'Brian's knee like he'd touched something hot.

O'Brian felt like punching the desk in frustration. The first half-way decent conversation he'd had with Valenti in a month and this stupid kid had to break in on it.

"Nothin,' junior," he growled, rounding to face his temporary partner, who was grinning at them uncertainly with an aw-shucks innocence the mean streets of LA hadn't managed to extinguish yet. He was a cute enough kid in his way, O'Brian supposed, with his farm-raised, corn-fed strapping physique and seven perfect freckles across the bridge of his snub nose. Someday he would make some lucky girl very happy but for now he was driving O'Brian nuts.

"No, seriously, guys, is everything all right? You looked, uh, really serious so I though maybe we had a new case -- *partner.*" He nudged O'Brian playfully who nudged him back, maybe a little harder than was absolutely necessary.

"Nothin' going on over here but a personal conversation," he said pointedly. The last thing he needed right then was to have this numb-nuts reminding Valenti that he was stuck riding a desk while O'Brian was out on the streets without him. But from the look in his partner's cold brown eyes, it was too late.

"Actually, I really need to get back to work," Valenti said, looking pointedly at the spot on his desk where O'Brian's ass was planted. "Do you mind? I owe the Captain these reports by five."

"Why so early?" O'Brian asked angrily. "You been stayin' here to seven, eight o'clock every night, wearin' yourself out. Too tired to go out and have any fun. Too tired to..." He trailed off when he realized that both Valenti and Hicks were staring at him.

"Hey, you guys go out together every night, don't you?" Hicks said, staring between the two of them. "I heard you two were tight, but, man -- spending that much time with your coworkers has got to be kind of tiring."

"More so lately than usual," Valenti said through gritted teeth. "Detective O'Brian, would you *please* move your ass off my desk so I can finish these?"

"Not until you tell me why you're wrappin' it up early tonight," O'Brian declared stubbornly. "Is it because..." His heart jumped suddenly in his chest as hope flooded him. "Because tonight it's uh, almost exactly one year?"

"One year?" Valenti looked at him blankly.

"Yeah, you know, one year since The RamJack." O'Brian lifted an eyebrow pointedly. Surely his partner hadn't forgotten their one-year anniversary, which was coming up on December fifth. It was kind of nice that it was near Christmas, O'Brian mused. Back at the time they had been undercover, they had been too focused on their goal of taking down drug kingpin Vincent Conrad to consider the season. But this year O'Brian was already thinking about what he could get his partner for a present -- if he remembered to show up for the celebration, that is.

"Oh, man, I heard about that RamJack thing!" Hicks exclaimed, breaking his train of thought. "Wasn't that the case where you guys --"

"Busted the biggest drug ring in the state?" Valenti interrupted him smoothly.

"Exactly," O'Brian said. "So that's why you're getting' off early, right? So we can celebrate?"

"Not exactly." Valenti sighed loudly. "I'm going to the Christmas benefit tonight for All Children's Hospital. Captain Harris asked me to bring the check the Metro PD raised to the chairman of their board and represent the department. Is that *okay* with you?" He voice dripped sarcasm.

"Fine." O'Brian slid off the desk and tried for a nonchalant tone of voice. "So, you bringin' a date? One of..." He cleared his throat and cast a quick glance at Hicks who was still following their conversation avidly. "One of the girls from the typing pool, maybe?"

Valenti shot him a glare. "So what if I am?"

O'Brian just looked at him, unable to keep the hurt off his face. Finally his partner relented.

"No," he said sullenly, crossing his arms over his chest. "The Captain only had one ticket. So I'm going solo. Anyway, it's not like I want to be handcuffed to some good looking bubblehead all night." Inexplicably his brown eyes flickered up to the uncomprehending Hicks for a second, before shifting back to the paperwork on his desk.

O'Brian felt a sudden loosening in the muscles of his chest. Thank God Valenti was going solo. Lately he'd been wondering if the extra conflict he sensed within his partner was an attraction to someone else. Maybe another guy on the force. Or even worse, Valenti might have decided to go back to the ladies. There wasn't much O'Brian could do about that -- he had the wrong kind of equipment for that kind of competition. *Like taking a vaulting pole to a breast-stroke event*, he thought wryly. But the way Valenti had phrased it -- being handcuffed to some good looking bubblehead all night -- now, that hurt. Was that what he thought of O'Brian now? *Wait a minute...*he thought. *Being hand-cuffed...*suddenly an idea was born.

"So you're gonna be at the benefit how long?" he asked casually, pretending to study his fingernails. From the corner of his eye he saw his partner giving him a suspicious look but at least Valenti answered.

"The benefit starts at seven and goes to midnight," he said shortly. "Satisfied?"

"No." O'Brian smirked at his partner. "But I will be, I promise you that, babe. See ya." And he headed out of the bullpen with Hicks trailing him like a lost puppy dog. Nothing against the kid but O'Brian was going to be damn glad to shake him -- he was tired of playing babysitter. But until Valenti came off desk duty, he was stuck with him.

"Hey, Detective O'Brian, it's too bad Detective Valenti can't go out with you tonight."

"Yeah, too bad," O'Brian agreed distractedly.

"Do you wanna go grab a cold one with me instead when we get off?" Hicks ventured hopefully.

O'Brian looked back to see that Valenti was watching them with narrowed eyes. Thinking it was the perfect opportunity to throw a little dirt on the trail, O'Brian nodded. "Sure, kid. Name the time and place." Of course when his trainee partner had done just that and he was sure they were clear of Valenti's sharp hearing, O'Brian shook his head and looked doubtful. "Oh, don't know if I can make that -- it's kinda far for me and I just now remembered I was gonna come in early and do some paperwork tomorrow."

"But tomorrow's Saturday," Hicks protested. "You never do paperwork on the weekends unless Captain Harris forces you to."

"Well, I'm making an exception. Don't worry about it." O'Brian patted the kid on the cheek and walked off. Mission accomplished. Now he just had to work out the details of his plan for that night...

Chapter Two

The scrape of his tennis shoes against the steps of the convention center shook the memory of that afternoon at the Metro and brought O'Brian back to the here and now. He hadn't dressed up for the benefit and he knew he was going look out of place with the ritzy crowd inside but he didn't care. His skin-tight jeans and T-shirt when everyone else was wearing tails and tuxes was all part of the strategy. Whistling, he made his way through the massive lobby, tastefully decorated in red, green, and gold to the place where the All Children's benefit was taking place.

"Sorry, sir, no one's allowed without an invitation." The beefy guard at the door of the grand ballroom reminded O'Brian of Conrad's goons at the RamJack -- each one uglier than the last and all of them built like tanks.

"Here's my invitation." He shoved his gold detective's badge under the guy's nose, pleased as always to see the instant change it engendered.

"Uh, sorry, officer." The guard looked sullen now, his authority trumped by O'Brian's badge. "Go on in. They're still just doing cocktails, anyway."

"As a matter of fact, a *cock*tail is right up my alley." O'Brian flashed him a toothy grin and shoved open the double doors to find himself in the middle of what looked like a best dressed contest.

Women in silk and satin evening gowns and elegant up-dos mingled with men wearing tuxes and bow ties, all of them sipping tall, slender flutes of champagne carried on trays by white-aproned waiters. O'Brian grabbed a flute off a passing tray and downed it in one long swallow, then put it on another tray as a second waiter passed by. Ignoring the confused and disdainful looks he was getting from the well dressed benefit attendees all around him, he began threading his way through the crowd, looking for Valenti.

It didn't take him long to see his partner, standing head and shoulders above the other men in the room at the far end of the ballroom. He was standing next to the tastefully decorated Christmas tree, deep in conversation with an older, distinguished looking man with iron-gray hair and serious eyes. O'Brian didn't waste time looking at the other man though; he had eyes for nobody but Valenti. Standing there cool and distinguished in his fitted black tux, his tall partner looked every inch a rich, refined gentleman, reminding O'Brian again of their time spent undercover when his partner had played "Daddy" to O'Brian's "boy." Damn, it had really pissed him off that he had to be the "boy" at first, but he had certainly made the most of the role, tormenting his sexually frustrated partner until both of them lost it completely.

Just thinking of the very first time they had ever made love -- the first time they had ever fucked, to put it crudely -- put a lump in O'Brian's pants. The way Valenti had been all over him, the things he had whispered to his partner to enflame him to action. *Do it, Valenti. Can't wait any longer. Need to have you in me. Need to feel you fuck me.* O'Brian's own words came back to haunt him as he watched his partner, his best friend, his lover conversing quietly in the crowded ballroom. God, he wanted this man so badly he ached! And yet lately it felt like Valenti was slipping further and further away from him.

Well, not any more, O'Brian decided. Squaring his shoulders, he pressed through the crowd and wound up right behind his partner.

"...a very important contribution," the gray-haired man was saying, and Valenti nodded.

"Absolutely, and the PD is more than glad to help, Chairman Tanner. I --"

"Excuse me." O'Brian tapped his partner on the shoulder and Valenti turned, a surprised look on his face. "O'Brian," he said blankly. "What are you doing here dressed like that?"

"Sorry I didn't have time to put on a monkey suit," O'Brian said sarcastically. "But I came here in kinda a hurry. Sorry to drag you away from your fancy party but we have a situation to deal with."

"What? What are you talking about?" Valenti looked confused as O'Brian hooked him by the elbow and began pulling him through the crowd. "That was Chairman Tanner, the head of the hospital board of directors," he hissed at O'Brian as they wove through the richly dressed crowd.

"I don't care if he was Santa Claus and the pope all wrapped up in one," O'Brian growled, still tugging his partner towards the exit. "You're comin' with me."

"But why?" Valenti continued to protest, but at least his feet were still moving, a situation O'Brian didn't expect to last long. He tugged harder.

"It's urgent," he said vaguely. "And we're the only two guys on the force that can handle it. You gotta come with me, Valenti. And hurry!"

O'Brian kept dodging his partner's pointed questions until they were out in the parking area across from the convention center. But when it came to actually getting into O'Brian's '82 Cordoba, Valenti balked.

"Look, what is this all about?" he demanded for what felt like the fiftieth time. "And don't just tell me it's urgent -- I want to know where the hell we're going and what's going on."

"I'll tell you what's going on." O'Brian pushed his surprised partner up against the side of the car and grabbed both his arms.

Before Valenti knew what was happening, O'Brian had whipped out his silver police issue cuffs and had them fitted snugly around his partner's wrists.

"What the hell do you think you're doing?" Valenti stared down at his cuffed wrists in amazement. "Have you gone crazy?"

"You could say that," O'Brian said grimly. "Crazy or horny, one of the two. Either way, you're comin' with me."

"I am not." Valenti rattled the cuffs threateningly. "Get me out of these and let me go back to the benefit."

"Nope." O'Brian whipped a black bandana out of his hip pocket. Before Valenti could protest, he was blindfolded and in the front seat of the Cordoba, his hands folded neatly in his lap. O'Brian smiled as he shut the door on his dumbfounded partner. Nobody was better at "cuff 'em and stuff 'em" than he was -- Valenti ought to know that by now. But his partner had other things on his mind than O'Brian's law enforcement prowess at the moment -- like escape.

"You let me out of here right now," he snarled as O'Brian started the engine. "Or I swear to God --"

"Nick," O'Brian interrupted him gently. "Do I hafta gag you too?"

"I --" Valenti began but O'Brian reached over and cupped his partner's strong chin in one hand, tracing Valenti's full mouth with his thumb.

"Don't make me do it, Nick," he murmured. "Not when I can think of so many better ways to use that beautiful mouth."

Valenti was abruptly silent and O'Brian could feel his partner's hot breath against his fingers as he drove. Just touching Valenti again, no matter how little, made him hard as a brick. Suddenly the distance between the convention center and his apartment seemed a lot longer. But he knew when he got there, he was going to give his partner an evening to remember -- he just hoped Valenti would forgive him afterwards.

Chapter Three

The minute O'Brian got his silent partner out of the door and into his apartment, he dragged Valenti directly into the bedroom. He'd had other things planned, romantic things, but right that minute he wasn't feeling the least bit romantic. His cock was aching with an entire month of pent up desire and he didn't have time for hearts and flowers.

"O'Brian, what the hell --?" Valenti began again as O'Brian slapped the bedroom door closed behind them.

"Shut up," O'Brian growled. He pushed his partner down on the bed and uncuffed Valenti's right wrist just long enough to strip off the beautifully tailored tux jacket and the crisp white dress shirt underneath. He ran both hands over the hard, muscular planes of his partner's smooth, brown chest, reveling in the feel of the masculine body under his fingertips. Gently he pinched the small, flat, copper-colored disks of Valenti's nipples, then leaned down to lap at one eagerly until his partner hissed with the hot sensation.

"O'Brian...!" he gasped. Far from slowing him down, the tortured moan pushed all O'Brian's buttons. He sucked at the other nipple, stopping to nip it sharply and then lapped it gently to ease the sharp little pain. The long, lean body writhed under his assault.

God, but his partner's skin tasted good—hot and salty, with just a hint of bitterness. Valenti had a warm, earthy scent O'Brian associated with fucking. This was the scent that had filled his senses the first time Valenti rode him, filled him with his long cock, fucked him until he came deep in O'Brian's body. This was the scent of his partner, his friend, his lover -- it was desire and need and coming home all at once and it had been too damn long since O'Brian had gotten close enough to fill his lungs with it.

"God!" Valenti, still blindfolded, was shivering with the hot feeling of being licked and stroked all over but O'Brian wasn't done yet -- not by a long shot. Grabbing Valenti's wrists, he brought them up to the top of the big brass bed. Then he snapped them closed again, effectively trapping his partner in a helpless position with his arms over his head.

"What are you going to do to me?" Valenti's voice was rough with fear and desire.

"Have you ever heard of the Spanish Inquisition?" O'Brian asked, not bothering to answer the question.

"Huh?" Valenti moved his head blindly, the black bandana still obscuring his vision. "The Spanish Inquisition?"

"You oughta know this stuff, *Corazón*," O'Brian mocked him, using his abuelita's nickname, the one he knew Valenti hated. "It's in your blood. Anyway, what it boils down to is during the Spanish Inquisition the bad guy priests tortured people until they told the truth."

"So what does that have to do with this?" Valenti demanded, rattling the handcuffs against the brass headboard.

"Actually, a helluva lot, babe," O'Brian told him, going to work on his partner's black dress pants. "See, I may not be a priest, but I *am* the bad guy in this situation. And I'm gonna torture you until you tell me what the hell has been bothering you lately. Why you've been givin' me the cold shoulder, why you're always too busy to come over or go out after work, but mostly why we haven't *fucked* in over a month. Got that?" He stripped off his partner's pants and underwear, taking the shoes and socks along with them and leaving Valenti nude on the dark blue bedspread.

"O'Brian, this is crazy!" Valenti protested.

"No, the way you've been actin' is crazy." O'Brian toed off his shoes but kept the rest of his clothes on. He liked the idea of having his partner naked and helpless under him and wanted the psychological edge of wearing clothes while Valenti had none.

"O'Brian, I --"

"What's been botherin' you, Nick?" O'Brian straddled his partner's lean hips and settled himself comfortably so that the thick bulge at the crotch of his jeans was rubbing directly against Valenti's already half-hard cock. Valenti groaned at the contact as O'Brian rubbed against him, their shafts grinding together through the layer of denim.

"Don't know...don't know what you're talking about," he gasped.

"Oh, I think you do." Reaching down, O'Brian shifted so he could wrap his fingers around the long, pulsing shaft. Slowly he stroked from the root up to the flaring head. Precum was already beading at the tip of Valenti's cock and O'Brian captured some with his thumb, using it for lubrication on the next long, slow stroke. It still amazed him that he wanted another man this much, that his partner's long, lean, muscular body could make him hotter than any curvy naked woman ever had. He knew why it was, though -- he and Valenti connected on much more than the physical plane. They had a bond so deep and wide nothing could break it -- not even Valenti's little secret, whatever it was.

He admired the way Valenti's muscles shifted under his smooth, tanned skin as he writhed on the bed, loved the crisp black hair that lay in disarray across his high forehead, the red lips, open in a harsh, panting moan. But most of all O'Brian loved the feel of his partner's thick cock in his hand, the tender, vulnerable sac that O'Brian knew exactly how to tickle to make Valenti groan. He'd never dreamed that having the same equipment as your lover could be such an advantage before he and Valenti had taken the next step in their relationship. Had never dreamed he could get so much pleasure from the feel of another man's cock in his hand, in his mouth, from the taste of another man's cum on his tongue.

"Remember the first time you jerked me off, Valenti?" he asked, still stroking his partner's aching shaft. "That Wankathon contest at The RamJack?"

"God, yes!" Valenti groaned as O'Brian continued to fist him.

"I remember the way you took charge of me," O'Brian said, lost in the memory. "The way you made me hold still while you jerked me off. You stroked me just like this..." He demonstrated with another long, slow caress of his partner's hard cock until Valenti was panting. "Made me come so hard I saw stars," O'Brian told him. "Remember that?"

"How...how could I forget it?" Valenti asked.

"I dunno. How could you? Tonight is practically our anniversary. A year ago tonight you were fucking my brains out at The RamJack," O'Brian reminded him. "And yet you'd rather go to some damn stupid benefit than spend the night celebrating with me."

"Is that what this is all about?" Valenti demanded.

"It's more than that and you know it." O'Brian gave him another long, slow stroke.

Valenti gasped and tried to sit up, only to be jerked back by the short chain between the cuffs. He growled in frustration. "Look, uncuff me or at least take off this damn blindfold and we'll talk about it."

"No can do, babe. Not the cuffs, at least. But here." Leaning over, O'Brian jerked the black bandana off his partner's head, freeing Valenti's eyes at last. He saw the anger in their deep brown depths, but he saw the hunger too. That was the emotion he wanted to feed.

"Look, O'Brian," Valenti began angrily as soon as his eyes adjusted to the dim light.

"No, *you* look," O'Brian told him. Leaning over, he started at the root of his partner's throbbing erection and licked a long, hot trail right up to the broad, mushroom-shaped head.

"God!" Suddenly the tension in the body under O'Brian's changed as Valenti's body moved seamlessly from anger to arousal.

"Remember, Nicky?" O'Brian whispered, holding eye contact with his partner as he blew a cool stream of air along the wet trail he'd licked. "Remember the first time I ever sucked your cock?" He leaned down and placed a hot, open-mouthed kiss on the broad head of Valenti's shaft. "Didn't know what the hell I was doin'," he continued as his partner watched, wide-eyed, no longer interrupting. "I only knew I wanted to taste you, wanted to feel your thick cock fucking my mouth." He lapped at the tip of Valenti's cock, savoring the salty, slightly bitter flavor of his partner's precum. "Wanted to suck you until I felt you shoot your cum down my throat," he murmured, locking eyes with his partner again.

"I remember the way you bucked your hips, the way you thrust up to meet me. I could feel your hands on me in the dark -- strokin' my hair, reachin' down to touch my face while I sucked you, like you couldn't quite believe I was really doin' it and you had to make sure. And then when you finally let go, finally started fuckin' your thick cock between my lips until you shot down my throat -- damn, it was the hottest thing I'd ever experienced. The best sex I'd ever had and it was *me suckin' another guy's cock*. You know how deep our connection has to be to make that possible?" O'Brian demanded. "Me, who beat up every dumb jock in high school for callin' me 'fag' cause I was too little and too cute?"

"Sean..." Valenti shook his head. "I just thought..."

"You just thought you could forget all about that -- about us -- for the past month. Thought you could skip the one-year anniversary of the time we spent at The RamJack. Thought you could keep secrets from me and get away with it. Didn't you?"

O'Brian demanded. "Well I'm here ta let you know you can't, babe." Leaning down, he lapped at the pearl of precum decorating his partner's throbbing crown once more before taking the long, thick cock completely down his throat.

It had taken almost a year, but O'Brian had gotten very good at deep-throating. He sucked and swallowed his partner's shaft, taking it deeper and deeper until he was tasting the river of warm, salty precum at the back of his throat instead of across his tongue. If anyone had ever told him before The RamJack that being able to suck cock correctly would be one of his proudest achievements, O'Brian would have laid the bastard out cold. And yet, it was true. Valenti's passionate moans and the convulsive shivers of pleasure he felt running through the long frame beneath him was worth every minute he'd spent attaining this strangely enjoyable skill. He only wished that he could have left at least one of Valenti's hands uncuffed. There was no greater pleasure than feeling his partner's big, warm hand carding through his hair and caressing his face while O'Brian sucked his thick cock, urging him to come.

"God! Oh, God, Sean! Gonna...can't help it! Gonna..."

O'Brian felt the big muscles of his partner's thighs turn to iron under his palms, and then Valenti's lean hips bucked upwards helplessly as the electric spasm of orgasm wracked him. Instead of pulling back, O'Brian sucked harder, taking Valenti even deeper into his throat, working for the hot flood of cum he knew was on its way.

He wasn't disappointed. Valenti had always been a big producer and it had taken some time to get used to swallowing his load. To get used to the idea of swallowing *any* man's load, O'Brian thought, as he drank the salty/bitter tide thirstily. And yet the pleasure he saw on his partner's face as he sucked out every last drop of cum did more for him than seeing a pretty woman sucking his own cock ever had. It was the act itself -- an act of love, an expression of the bond between them that got him every time.

That and the fact that he loved making his straight-laced partner lose control.

"O'Brian...I can't believe..." Valenti was limp, his brown eyes melting with emotion.

"Believe it, babe," O'Brian said shortly. "And now you better get ready to be fucked. Suckin' your cock has me wantin' you so bad I can't see straight."

Valenti went a little pale beneath his natural tan. "God, Sean, I don't know. It's been over a month since we..."

"I know exactly how long it's been," O'Brian growled. His cock was snarling in his jeans for release, and he pulled his T-shirt over his head and unsnapped his fly. "It's been way too long since I've buried my cock inside you and fucked you hard and long. I'm gonna ride your ass tonight, Nicky, and you're gonna love every minute of it."

"God, when you talk that way..." Valenti closed his eyes briefly and took a deep, shuddering breath before looking at O'Brian again. "How do you want me?" he asked, his deep voice soft and tense. "Oh my hands and knees? The way we did it that first time?"

"Want you just like you are right now," O'Brian assured him. Suddenly his heart swelled with love for his partner, this man who was so willing to open his heart, to open his body. Who was willing to allow O'Brian to penetrate him, to fuck him and come in him despite the fact that neither of them had ever done anything remotely like this before they had taken their friendship to the next level. He leaned over and kissed Valenti long and slow, just like he'd been dying to do for the entire last month. Parting the soft red lips, he invaded his partner's mouth, feeding Valenti the taste of his own cum on his tongue, making the other man moan with the intensity of the kiss.

At last he drew back and fumbled in the nightstand beside him for the lube. They'd come a long way since the jar of Vaseline he'd used the first time he fucked Valenti. The lube was cool and smooth and allowed for easier access to resistant flesh.

Speaking of easier access, Valenti had spread his thighs and damned if his cock wasn't half hard again. He could say what he wanted about it being a long time since they'd done this but O'Brian knew how much his partner needed to be fucked -- almost as much as O'Brian needed to fuck him.

"That's right, babe," he murmured as he spread the cool, slick lube over the tight, tender entrance to his partner's body. "Open up for me. I know how bad you need ta be fucked. And I know you want me to fuck you." O'Brian pressed two fingers into Valenti's body, scissoring them gently to spread him wide enough for his cock.

"Yeah, I need it," Valenti almost snarled, his brown eyes submissive and angry at the same time. "But I think you better remember that next time it might be you in these handcuffs, *partner*, and I'm not going to forget the way you held me down and fucked me like a helpless girl."

O'Brian's heart leaped at the words "next time." He was glad to hear that his partner wasn't planning on leaving him for good after this was over. "Nicky," he said sincerely, "You c'n hang me upside down and do Chinese water torture on me if you want to later. But for right now, I feel like I'm gonna explode if I don't get inside you soon. It's been so damn long since we touched each other I'm achin' all over to be with you."

Valenti's eyes softened and he spread his legs wider as O'Brian continued to stretch him. "You always did need it more than me," he murmured, arching his back and gasping as O'Brian's probing fingers hit the sweet spot just over his prostate. "Even...even back when we were still dating women, you couldn't go a week without getting some."

"Nice of you to remember that now, after a month of cuttin' me off," O'Brian growled. He pressed harder, deliberately rubbing over the sensitive area inside Valenti's body until his partner's eyes rolled up in his head and he groaned appreciatively. "But never mind about that," he continued. "'Cause I think you're ready now. Ready to get fucked, babe."

Before Valenti could reply, O'Brian spread his partner's legs even wider and found Valenti's tight rosebud with the blunt tip of his cock. Slowly he began to thrust, breaching the tight ring of muscle as Valenti groaned and tried to be open enough for the invasion.

O'Brian got the head in and then he had to stop. Just that simple touch, the feel of his shaft crowning inside his partner's body was almost too much after such a long, dry time of wanting. *God, babe, love you! Love you so much!* he thought, clenching his jaw and tensing his lower body to keep from coming. He didn't want to reach the peak until he was buried to the hilt in his lover's body, until they were completely and totally one.

"What...what are you waiting for?" Valenti gasped. "And engraved invitation?" The brown eyes were on fire now, blazing with a need that fully matched O'Brian's own. "Come on, damnit," he growled. "Fuck me!"

Valenti didn't have to ask twice. With one long, hard thrust O'Brian entered his partner's body, claiming him, marking him as thoroughly and completely as he had the first time he fucked Valenti.

"God!" Valenti's hips shot off the mattress and for a moment it almost looked like he was fighting not to try and get away. Then he took a deep, shuddering breath and opened his eyes, which he'd squeezed close in pain and pleasure.

"You okay? Want me to stop?" His cock still throbbing angrily, O'Brian forced himself to hold still even though every instinct he had cried out for him to thrust. He watched his partner with concern. No matter how angry and conflicted the two of them might be, Valenti was the person he loved most in the world, and he would die before hurting him.

"Hell no, I don't want you to stop," Valenti blazed, surprising him. "Fuck me, babe. I want to feel you in me and when you're done, I want to know I've been fucked. Fill me up, do it!"

"Oh, you're gonna know, all right," O'Brian promised. Drawing back till only the head of his cock was buried in the tight confines of his partner's body, he thrust back in again, filling his partner to the limit and beyond, watching the pain and pleasure cross the dark, mobile face he loved so much as he poured himself into Valenti's body.

"God, Sean!" Valenti gasped, his voice hoarse with emotion. "You're in me so deep!"

"I'll show you deep," O'Brian growled. He plunged forward again, relishing the tight, hot, velvety feel of the inside of his partner's body clinging to every inch of his shaft, igniting every single nerve in his cock. God but Valenti was tight -- it had been so long since they'd fucked his partner was practically a virgin again.

Valenti bucked up against him, a whole host of emotions flitting across his dark face. Love, anger, need, lust...O'Brian watched them all come and go as he lost himself in the pleasure of filling his partner, of taking another man's body, of fucking Valenti senseless.

He set up a rhythm of slow, deliberate, almost brutally deep thrusts, rubbing hard over and over Valenti's sweet spot as his partner writhed under him, groaning and cursing with the intense, almost unbearable pleasure/pain. Valenti's cock was full again and O'Brian reached down to palm it as he continued to pound into his partner's open, willing body. He could feel the tidal wave of pleasure coming, building like slow electricity at the base of his spine, and he wanted Valenti to come with him, just as he had the first time they'd fucked.

"God, Sean!" Valenti grabbed handfuls of the dark blue bedspread, his teeth clenched and his breath sobbing in his throat as O'Brian fisted his cock and pounded into him, owning him completely. "God, that's so incredible! Don't stop...don't stop! Love your cock inside me -- love to feel you fucking me!"

"Gonna come inside you," O'Brian promised breathlessly. His skin was slick with sweat and he was breathing like a bull and still he couldn't stop. Couldn't stop until he had put paid to this whole business by filling his partner's willing, unresisting body with his cum.

"Sean!" Valenti's darkly tanned skin was sheened lightly with sweat as well, and the chain of the cuffs was rattling in rhythm with O'Brian's thrusts as he pressed back against him, meeting O'Brian with everything he had. "God, do it!" he begged shamelessly. "Fuck me! Fill me up! Need you to fill me up so *bad*."

"Here it comes, babe," O'Brian gasped, the electric tingle of orgasm rolling up his spine. The slick heat of Valenti's inner muscles caressing his cock was too much -- too damn much to bear anymore. "Comin' right now. Want to feel you comin' with me."

OhGodohGodohGod. So good, so Goddamn good! O'Brian thought deliriously as the shattering wave overcame him. Feeling like his heart was going to explode, he pumped Valenti's long, thick shaft with one fist as he pressed hard, trying to get his own cock as deeply into his partner's beautiful, hot body as he could. Wanting to be one with Valenti in that special way that was only possible during this one brief instant.

With an inarticulate cry, Valenti came. O'Brian felt a hot wetness fountaining over his hand and then he was letting go too, pumping Valenti's body full of his cum, filling him up with an inexpressible relief, a pleasure so deep it bordered on pain.

"God, Nick," he groaned, holding still inside Valenti as the hot flood gushed out of him and into his partner, sealing their bond. "Love you so damn much, babe. Can't even tell you. Just...just love you so much." He held steady for a long moment and then sank down, his cheek pillowed on his partner's heaving chest.

"Love you too, Sean." Valenti's voice was hoarse from shouting but he sounded at peace for the first time in over a month.

O'Brian took a deep breath, feeling his heart rate begin to slow, and looked up. "You sure got a funny way of showin' it," he said mildly, giving his partner a doubtful grin.

Valenti shook his head. "I thought you were...that you weren't interested in me...in us anymore."

O'Brian had a feeling they were finally coming to the root of the problem that had been bothering his partner all along. "What the hell would give you a stupid idea like that?" he demanded, withdrawing carefully from Valenti's body and sitting back on his knees.

Valenti winced at the sudden withdrawal, then shrugged as well as he was able with his hands still cuffed over his head. "I don't know. The fact that I'm stuck behind that stupid desk all day long so I can't get your back on the streets. And..." He frowned and looked away. "That new partner of yours -- that Billy Hicks. I know it sounds stupid but I kept thinking that he was younger, that maybe you found him more desirable..."

"*What?*" O'Brian couldn't keep the disbelief out of his voice. "You thought *what?* That I'd want to be with that idiot kid instead of you?"

"Well, I --" Valenti began but O'Brian cut him off.

"Listen, partner," he said pointing a finger at Valenti's face and narrowing his eyes. "What the hell are you tryin' to say? That I'd leave you for somebody else? For another man? What do you think I am anyway, gay?"

"Uh..." Valenti shook his head as though trying to clear some faulty information. "Sean, I hate to point this out but you just gave me the best blowjob of my entire life and swallowed a load of my cum. Then you fucked me so hard I nearly passed out. Most people might consider that just a little bit 'gay.'"

"Well, I'm not most people." O'Brian folded his arms across his furry chest, still frowning. "And I don't consider myself gay, babe. I'm just in love with you. I don't even look at other guys that way. That would be just...*wrong*." He shook his head.

Valenti burst out laughing. "O'Brian, you never cease to amaze me. I guess I should have known better." His brown eyes filled with apology. "I mean, the way Hicks follows you around all over the place, the way he looks at you like you're some kind of rock star, I just assumed..."

O'Brian frowned at him. "We're gonna pass on the little talk about what happens when you *assume*," he said. "Since I think your ass is already gonna be sore for the foreseeable future." He ignored Valenti's wince and continued. "Why didn't you just ask?" he demanded. "Why did you just decide it was up to you to break us off? To end everything we have together? Ya know, Valenti, you're not just my lover..." He leaned forward and stroked the lean, tan cheek gently. "You're my partner and my best friend," he continued. "I *need* you."

"I need you too..." Valenti smiled at him, the first genuine smile O'Brian had seen from him since the whole rotten shooting incident had almost ruined their relationship over a month ago. "To uncuff me," his partner finished, still smiling. "Swear to God, O'Brian, my arms are about to fall off. Did you really have to resort to such extreme measures? Kidnapping me and cuffing me to the bed so you could fuck me senseless?"

"You tell me what I was supposed to do," O'Brian grumbled, reaching for the handcuff key, which lay on the night table beside the bed. "I tried bein' patient, but you just got further and further away. I tried sweet-talk but you wouldn't give me the time of day." He shrugged and unlocked the cuffs. "Under the circumstances I thought kidnappin' you and cuffing you to the bed was my only option. And I didn't fuck you senseless -- the exact opposite. I'd say I fucked some sense *into* you just now."

"Regardless, it was a pretty damn fine anniversary present." Valenti rubbed his wrists gingerly and then sank down in the bed, motioning for O'Brian to come join him.

"Didja ever stop to think that maybe it was an early Christmas present?" O'Brian yawned hugely as he settled his head on his lover's bicep. "And if you're good, there's plenty more like that comin' down the chimney just for you, Nicky."

"I don't know about that." Valenti winced. "Damn, I'm sore! I think this is going to be one time when I'm glad that Christmas comes but once a year."

"Yeah, but you already came twice tonight," O'Brian pointed out, with another yawn.

"I did." Valenti sounded thoughtful. "And that's why I think the next present should be for you, partner."

"Whatever you say," O'Brian mumbled, his eyelids heavy with sleep. "Lemme catch a quick catnap and we can keep givin' each other presents all night long."

The last thing he heard as he drifted off was his partner's low chuckle against the side of his face. He felt utterly spent but in a happy, warm, contented way as sleep dragged him under.

Detective Sean O'Brian had finally had enough.

ᘓTHE ENDᘔ

Evangeline Anderson

Evangeline Anderson is a registered MRI tech who would rather be writing. She is thirty-something and lives in Florida with a husband, three cats and a college-age sister but no kids because enough is enough already. She had been writing dirty stories for her own gratification for a number of years before it occurred to her to try and get paid for it. To her delight, she found it was actually possible to get money for having a dirty mind and she has been writing steadily ever since.

You can find Evangeline Anderson on the Web at www.evangelineanderson.com.

Printed in the United States
211337BV00001B/18/P